W9-ACR-945

# The Farnsworth $core

A JOAN KAHN BOOK

*Books by Rex Burns*

THE FARNSWORTH SCORE
THE ALVAREZ JOURNAL

# The Farnsworth Score

## Rex Burns

ASBURY PARK PUBLIC LIBRARY
ASBURY PARK, NEW JERSEY

HARPER & ROW, PUBLISHERS
New York, Hagerstown, San Francisco,
London

# A HARPER NOVEL OF SUSPENSE

THE FARNSWORTH SCORE. Copyright © 1977 by Rex Raoul Stephen Sehler Burns. All rights reserved. Printed in the United States of America. No part of this book may be used or reproduced in any manner whatsoever without written permission except in the case of brief quotations embodied in critical articles and reviews. For information address Harper & Row, Publishers, Inc., 10 East 53rd Street, New York, N.Y. 10022. Published simultaneously in Canada by Fitzhenry & Whiteside Limited, Toronto.

FIRST EDITION

*Designed by Dorothy Schmiderer*

---

Library of Congress Cataloging in Publication Data

Burns, Rex.
  The Farnsworth Score.
  I. Title: The Farnsworth score.
PZ4.B96835Far    [PS3552.U7325]    813'.5'4    76–26263
ISBN 0–06–010573–9

---

77 78 79 80 10 9 8 7 6 5 4 3 2 1

*To: Chris, Erik, and Andrew*

# The Farnsworth $core

# 1

Gabriel Wager sensed something in the way Suzy, the secretary for the Organized Crime Division, glanced up as he came in.

"What's wrong?"

"Have you seen Sergeant Johnston yet?" Her blue eyes were the only part of her face anyone would notice. Right now they were wide with excitement.

"Is he looking for me?"

"You, Ashcroft, Hansen—anybody!"

"He in here?" Wager started toward the plywood cubicle of the sergeant's office.

"No, he's with the inspector right now."

Wager glanced down the hall and saw that the inspector's door was closed. "What's the trouble?"

She peeked out and around the pale green plywood that

screened the narcotics section from the other units in the division; throughout the cluttered second floor of the old brick building typewriters rattled with morning briskness; an occasional electronic snap opened the day's first radio traffic. "You know the Farnsworth case?"

"Was that the one Rietman was assigned to?"

"I think he blew it."

"Rietman?" That didn't sound right. "Why?"

"I'm not sure. When Inspector Sonnenberg came in this morning, he was mad! He asked for Detective Rietman's folder and called Sergeant Johnston in."

"Really pissed?"

"Mad," she said firmly.

Rietman. In the year the young detective had been with the Organized Crime Division, he'd done a steady job, and it didn't sound like him to foul up. But it could happen—it did happen. God knows Wager had dropped his share of cases; it took some of that to train an officer. But it still wasn't pleasant to think of. "Well, if it's bad, we'll hear about it."

"*You* will." There were many things Suzy wasn't told.

Wager sat at his desk and read through last night's messages before turning to the unfinished reports and the queries from other agencies. He was in the middle of a *modus operandi* description on a series of drugstore robberies in neighboring Jefferson County when he heard Sergeant Johnston's voice say, "Yes, sir," at the inspector's door. Wager paused. If it was good news, Johnston would come to his desk; if it was bad, he'd phone. The telephone buzzed and Suzy said, "Gabe, for you."

"Good morning, Ed."

"How'd you know it was me?"

"I'm a detective."

"Oh. Can I see you for a minute?"

"Be right there." He went the five steps to the unit sergeant's office; behind his desk with its carefully stacked papers,

2

Johnston sat, balding head sinking slightly in front of the round shoulders.

"Gabe, we've been thrown for a loss." Ed had recently become a Broncos fan and was replacing administrative jargon with football slang. He was the team quarterback; the inspector was the coach; Gabe, Rietman, Ashcroft, and Hansen were the front four. "You know anything about the Farnsworth case?"

"Only rumor, nothing official. The subject's cocaine, and the Drug Enforcement Administration's the primary agency."

"Right—D.E.A. was calling the signals. They borrowed Rietman to act as buyer. How well do you know him?"

"He's pretty new—we didn't work together. But I never heard anything against him, either."

Johnston nodded and gazed at the painted plywood that gave his desk a little privacy but blocked any fresh air that sneaked through the old square windows. Wager preferred his desk out in the open. Actually, he would prefer no desk at all; but half of a detective's job was keeping records and files, and what couldn't be kept in memory was stored in the desk—along with the piles of forms that someone kept manufacturing but no one seemed to care about. "Rietman set up the deal and it went down, and they made a clean bust—possession, conspiracy, and sale."

"And?"

Johnston paused for effect. "And they lost the ball on the one-yard line!"

Wager blinked; it wouldn't be thrown out of court for a half-assed reason. The D.E.A. people were experienced agents, and would have noted the chain of evidence, exact times and locations of contacts, key conversations that revealed the suspect's intent to sell narcotics. And they had all testified enough not to try any nonsense on the witness stand. "Why?"

"The D.E.A. people say that Rietman messed up on the field test. The Colorado Bureau of Investigation's lab reported that the stuff was lactose. So no case. D.E.A. thinks that the suspects were setting a phony deal to find out if the buyers were straight, and that Rietman ran a bad test, thought it was presumptive positive, and gave the bust sign. Six months they been trying to lay a deal on Farnsworth. And when they finally get it . . ." The balding head dipped and wagged again.

"Did he?"

"Did he what?"

"The field test—did Rietman run a bad one?"

"The agents ended up with two and a half pounds of lactose. It ain't against the law to sell lactose."

"What's Rietman say?"

"He swears he did it right. He said he'd take a lie-detector test."

"That won't mean a thing if he really thinks he did it right."

"I know. But D.E.A.'s been all over us about it; the inspector's already put Rietman back in uniform."

"That's pretty heavy for Rietman."

"Tell that to D.E.A. They think he should of been canned." Johnston picked up a leaf of paper from one neat pile and placed it on another, neater pile. "The inspector feels that since it was our man, our agency's responsible."

"Oh?" Wager smelled it coming, "And now he wants us to sweep up the shit?"

Ed patted the few pale red hairs into place on the center of his freckled scalp. "D.E.A.'s handed us the ball. Let's see if the inspector's free."

He was. Wager trailed after Sergeant Johnston into the tiny office crowded with captain's chairs and a large clean desk; one wall held a hundred or so green volumes of the *Modern Federal Practice Digest.* It was the only office on the O.C.D. floor with a door and without a coffee cup; instead of the usual comic signs and posters about pigs and complaint forms, it had organization charts on the wall: "The Chicago Family," "The

4

Miami Family." But there was one other desk without cartoons and jokes on the walls: Wager's. Inspector Sonnenberg licked a dark brown cigar and lit it with one of the fireplace matches sprouting from a water glass on his desk. "Did Sergeant Johnston tell you about the famous Farnsworth fiasco?"

"Yes, sir."

He rolled the cigar slightly for an even burn; the inspector seemed to get more pleasure from lighting one than from smoking it. "Farnsworth's still working in Boulder County. He thinks nobody can touch him."

Wager was silent. Beside him, he heard Sergeant Johnston shift slightly on the unpadded wooden chair.

"I just came from a meeting with the D.E.A. people and the District Attorney. D.E.A.'s laying all sorts of nonsense at our door—they're using Rietman as an excuse to cover some of their own foul-ups. And they told the D.A. that they're pulling back from Farnsworth because of us."

"Yes, sir."

"The D.A. wants us to go after him." One puff. Two. "To save face. If we can get him, we'll have some leverage where we need it."

"You're right, Inspector," said Johnston. "If we could score on this one . . . !"

Wager listened and nodded and hoped it wouldn't be him. It had been a long time since he had gone undercover, but just the memory still wearied him. And that was three—Lord, four —years ago. He was getting too old for that kind of crap; there was too much crap an undercover man had to swallow. He hoped to God it wouldn't be him.

"Does anybody up in Boulder or Nederland know you?"

It was him. Wager slid the faces, names, aliases he'd dealt with in the past five or six years through his memory. None of them hung up on either town's name. But the inspector wouldn't know that; neither would Johnston. He could just say

5

yes and it would be someone else. All it took was a little lie that would never be found out. It would be so easy just to nod yes. "Not that I know of."

Sonnenberg's cigar glowed slightly. "Do you want to go under?"

No. The playacting took too much patience, too much energy. It was too hard to pretend any more. He was a cop and he liked it that way. "Do you really need me?"

"I understand that Farnsworth likes to work with Chicanos. He plays at being a revolutionary type. His mistress is a Chicano."

Chicana—the female form was Chicana. And there was nothing that wore on Wager more than a kid who had all the answers and no sense. "I've got a few things that'll have to be covered."

"No problem, Gabe," said Johnston. "We can split your load between Ashcroft and Hansen. Hell, you've substituted for them enough times."

"And I want somebody who can build a good case," said Sonnenberg.

The inspector was right: he was good. Wager nodded.

"Fine. Sergeant, let's make up a jacket for him—make him from, ah . . ."

"Texas. A lot of Hispanos come up from Texas."

"Good thinking. That's far enough away to be safe. I'll have to clear the Boulder County authorities, and you'll need a new government vehicle, as well as—" Sonnenberg cut himself short with a wave of the cigar, "You know your work."

Johnston said, "I'll take care of everything, sir."

Back at his desk, Wager told Suzy to say he was on assignment and to transfer routine calls to the sergeant. Then he dialed the D.E.A. number, asking for his ex-partner of a couple years past. Wager was grateful that the federal agency had left a local man in the region; usually they transferred their agents to distant stations "for security reasons." When Billy did go,

6

there wouldn't be anyone left in D.E.A. he could talk with.

"Gabe? How the hell are you doing?"

"Fine, Billy. How're the boys—Erik and Chris?"

"Bigger and sassier. When do we get together for that beer?"

"Anytime. Say, I need information on the Farnsworth case."

"Hey, man, what's happened to the old O.C.D? That kind of stuff didn't used to go down. Who is this Rietman guy?"

Wager shrugged. "He claims it tested positive."

"Too bad the lab said something else. I wasn't on the case, but I heard it was a bad scene. You picking it up?"

"I'm just trying to get a little information. You know how it is."

"Ha—yeah. I know you're a goddam Chicano clam."

"That's my barrio training; I don't spill to the fuzz."

"Ha. I'll see what I can do. You want the surveillance reports, too?"

"Everything."

"I'll phone you when I get it together."

His next call was to the Denver Police Department. Mark Rietman was on the street. Wager waited for the dispatcher to give him the message to call the O.C.D. number.

"This is Gabe, Mark. Can we meet somewhere?"

A brief silence. "I guess it's about that Farnsworth shit."

"Yes."

"What the hell's your angle?"

His angle was that he was a cop; Wager stifled his quick anger, but the lilt of his accent grew heavier. "The inspector, he wants us to keep on Farnsworth. How about meeting me at the Frontier when you go off duty?"

"Ah, shit on it. Yeah—O.K. I'll see you there around five."

He hung up.

"Gabe? If you have a minute, Sergeant Johnston wants to see you."

"Thanks, Suzy."

7

"Here's what I've got so far," the sergeant held out a folder for him to study; the label made use of his middle name: Villanueva, Gabriel. Johnston's penciled script outlined a history as close as possible to fact—place of birth, Houston, Texas; age, thirty-six; occupation, plasterer; marital status, separated; police record, one conviction in Brownsville, Texas, possession of marijuana. "What do you want for a place of residence?"

Already he felt it starting to close around him like the stiff manila of the folder; already the weariness of constantly remembering, of smiling when he wanted to puke, of betting his life he could make scum think he liked them. "My address."

Johnston wrote it down. "Anything else?"

He sighed and thought back to other undercover assignments, to other lives and pretenses of lives, dredging up the suspicions and questions, the assurances that had been bought in the past and those that hadn't been. "Better put me down as a burned-out junkie."

Johnston raised his eyebrows.

"That way I have an excuse for not shooting up if anybody tries to call me out."

"Right—good." He jotted it down.

"I'll need the right kind of vehicle, too. How about a VW or one of those Toyota pickups?"

"Not unless we have one in seized property. Otherwise it's got to be American-made. If the department buys anything but American-made, the local car dealers really raise hell."

"Too goddam bad Farnsworth doesn't have to buy American-made cocaine. Make it a little Chevy pickup. A used one and nothing fancy on it." He thought a minute or two. "No radio jack; Denver plates. And put a rifle rack across the rear window."

"I'll get the garage on it now."

He gazed at the skeleton of his new identity lying on the spread wings of the folder. He would be issued a driver's license

in Villanueva's name, a new Social Security card, Villaneuva's vehicle registration. On paper, it would be as complete as possible. But still the burden of fleshing out that skeleton weighed on him. Clothes. He'd have to get something convincing there, too. "What about contacts in Boulder? Who do I work with up there?"

"The inspector's making those arrangements. It'll be somebody in the sheriff's office."

"O.K." He bent the stiff folder closed. "Let me think things over. I'll let you know if I need anything else."

He sat at his desk and poured another cup of coffee from the tan thermos pitcher whose insides had gradually stained darker than the outer shell. And made the coffee taste stained, too. The folder, open again, gazed back at him; he let his mind pick here and there at the little pieces of flesh that would be molded into Gabriel Villanueva: dealer on the make, ex-Texas ranch hand, ex-plasterer, ex-husband; ex-cop, too, but that had to be buried very, very deep. He closed his eyes and pictured Villanueva, his clothes, his words, his manners. It was like pulling on a sweater that was too small, one that fit here and there but all too often caught at his freedom of motion and reminded him how tightly it bound. But it was he, and not the sweater, that had to adjust. It took a young excitement and eagerness to make that adjustment—eagerness, excitement, and youth that he no longer felt.

Suzy called to him, her hand across the telephone's mouthpiece: "Are you in? It's Agent Billington from D.E.A. He said you were expecting his call."

"Yes." He picked up his extension. "What do you have Billy?"

"A half-inch pile of reports. Do you want me to send them over, or do you want to pick them up?"

"I'll be right there."

Billy was at his desk, a large figure sloping over the littered

surface, lank blond hair dangling down to the coat collar that hitched up the back of his neck. He looked around as Wager came in.

"Hey, you tamale-rolling son of a bitch! Long time!"

"Up yours, too, gringo." Wager pumped his hand. It *had* been a long time.

"Here." Billy handed him a wad of legal-sized Xerox sheets. One group was labeled "SURVEILLANCE," the other "SPECIAL AGENTS REPORTS." "You want some lunch? You got time for that beer?"

"You're buying."

The state legislature was still in session; every restaurant around Capitol Hill would be jammed—the clerks and secretaries in the cheaper ones, lawmakers and lobbyists in the more expensive ones. "I know a great little Mexican place out on East Colfax. You like Mexican food?"

"You've never had any real Mexican food, white-eye."

"Wait'll you taste this chili pecosa, you phony wetback."

Billington drove; Wager studied the stack of s.a. reports. When they were seated at the small teetering table with its checkered oilcloth cover, Billington finally broke the silence. "Is Sonnenberg going after Farnsworth?"

"He is."

He poured a Coors. "Where do you fit?"

Wager couldn't help another sigh. "He wants me to make the contacts."

Billy whistled slightly. "You've been in the O.C.D. a long time. You're pretty well known."

Wager's shoulders bobbed. "Sonnenberg wants a solid case on him."

"Yeah, I see his point. Still." Billy sucked at the head on the beer. "Gabe, I'd be scared shitless if it was me. They ought to bring in a young guy, somebody from outside."

"That costs money. And I'm not a desk sergeant; it's part of the job."

"Still . . ." Then he, too, shrugged and buried what he was going to say in a mouthful of smoking rice. Wager could see Billy's thought: Gabe had been around; Gabe would know whether he could handle it or not; it was Gabe's business and nobody else's. Wager still liked the way his ex-partner thought.

He sawed into the cheese and shredded lettuce covering his Number 2 Special. God knew he did not like the idea of going under, but the inspector wanted him to and that was all there was to it.

Billy ordered two more Coors. "You want me to talk to any of our people who were on the case?"

"Not now. I'd just as soon keep it quiet that I'm involved at all. Like you say, I'm pretty well known."

"Farnsworth's just waiting for somebody else to come after him."

"¡Por supuesto! What dealer isn't?"

"I guess that's true enough."

He tapped the stack of sheets, "Your agent—Chandler—his report just covers the deal in Boulder. Does Farnsworth live there now?"

"Naw—up in Nederland. You know the place?"

It was a small mountain town about twenty miles west of Boulder, a collection of half a dozen bars, stores, tourist shops surrounded by vacation cabins and isolated houses scattered among the pines. In the summer, it was crowded with flatlanders and outsiders, the town trying in three short months to make enough tourist dollars to stretch through the winter. When the season ended, a new face would be a stranger there for a long time. "That will be a tough place to get into."

"That's why our people were so pissed when that asshole Rietman blew it. Six months it took Chandler to get solid up there."

"Any possibilities inside?"

"From all I heard, Farnsworth doesn't deal unless he's God damned sure of you. Most of the time he'll steer a buyer to somebody he supplies, and he supplies just the people he knows. *They* mostly supply just the people they know, and so on down to street level. That way, the street dealers take all the chances. But it doesn't do a damn bit of good to bust them."

It sounded very familiar. And very difficult. "How'd he get stung by Rietman and Chandler?"

"You'd better ask them. I wasn't in on it."

Wager nodded; he could guess anyway—a lot of time sitting, drinking, talking; a lot of small deals here and there; a lot of pure bullshit to have the people swallow Chandler's rap. And then Rietman is brought in for a buy that only Farnsworth can match. "Does your office have files on these people?"

"I'm sure we do. I'll get copies for you."

They finished, each trying to pay before the other could grab the check. Billy dropped him off at his car. "You sure you want to do this?"

"It's part of the job."

"Yeah. Well, take it easy, *amigo.*"

He watched Billy's gray Maverick disappear in the light traffic of a hot afternoon; then he sat for a few minutes in his own car and weighed the good and bad of talking to some of the Confidential Informants in his stable. Best not to, unless it was really necessary; he wanted to keep his name as far away as possible from anything to do with Farnsworth. If he did use C.I.s, they would have to be some other detective's. His own could guess too much, and he could not trust them to keep their mouths shut; there would be enough worry without that gnawing at the back of his mind.

Clothes—there was a little time before he met Rietman; enough time to get his costume together. Driving down Fourteenth to Larimer, he parked on one of the sun-softened asphalt lots that appeared whenever Urban Renewal tore down another building. Soon the featureless asphalt would be replaced by featureless concrete and glass; and in thirty years the area would have to be "renewed" again. Already he could hear the future slogans, "A New Denver for a New Century." And then they would try once more to make it look like half a dozen other cities back East.

A midsummer afternoon in Larimer Square: scattered groups of tourists in sunglasses jaywalking from boutique to shoppe, an occasional couple ducking out of a restaurant or swinging into a bar. At the glassed-in corner of the Royal Platte River Yacht Club, a handful of regulars leaned on wooden tables to sip beer and watch cars and tourists swirl past. Wager cut through a short arcade to a clothing store that was mercifully empty at the moment.

He told the girl clerk "Just looking," and began to browse the racks. Denim shirts with stitched patterns—a couple; maybe one or two of these T-shirts with names written on them: bicycle brands and tennis-shoe labels were in now. And a hat.

"How much is this one?"

She looked at the tag on the broad leather brim. Slightly shorter than his own five feet eight, she was in her early twenties, had the usual straight long hair and no make-up. She seemed very, very young. "Thirty-two fifty. We have some less expensive hats over here—the same model."

Wager looked at them, vaguely wondering what it was about him that always made clerks say they had something cheaper. "I like the first one better."

"Sure!" She hid her surprise and smiled when he put it on. "It makes you look a lot younger. Like a gaucho."

Sure it made him look younger. Like a goddam gaucho. In the trio of mirrors, his tired face peered back under the flat leather hat and stabbed him again with the thought of how much more make-believe was coming: light brown skin and dark eyes from his mother (may the earth rest lightly on her); his father's curling hair, black and still without gray. His father's square chin, too; but the lines around the eyes and mouth and the drooping mustache were his own. He replaced his sunglasses; he would have to bury that face, change it so that the mirror of the other people's eyes wouldn't see what he was. That hat was only the beginning. More face hair would complete it—a goatee, maybe, and let the sideburns grow longer. "Wrap it up."

"Sure."

The rest of the costume: worn Levis, he had; cowboy boots —if he was from Texas, he would need cowboy boots. They would be over three blocks at Western Wear. This time the clerk was male and he made a point of calling Wager "sir" and brought out several pairs of multicolored, hand-tooled boots, with flowers, horseheads, birds—everything except a mariachi band—carved on them.

"I want something plain enough to work in. Rough side out." They would look older, quicker. And were more comfortable; he hated the damned things anyway, and there was no sense suffering any more than he had to. He pried on three different sizes and took the largest.

"Anything else, sir?"

A wide leather belt and a big brass buckle with a steer's head on it. And a cheap straw cowboy hat to hang on the truck's rifle rack. He would do without the plastic Madonna for the dash or the little fringe of cotton balls over the front window; he was supposed to be a plasterer, not a bracero. But he would need a roll of toilet paper. West Texans always had a roll of toilet paper sitting up in the back window. He could think of a lot of reasons why.

At his car in the scorched parking lot, he locked the packages in the trunk and walked the block and a half to the Frontier. It was already starting to fill up with thirsty men just off work and a few broads with orange or platinum hair and high-pitched laughter who were probably just going to work. Wager said hello to Red, and the bartender flicked a busy hand in return. Some tourists who looked out of place were crammed into his favorite booth; Wager took a small open table near the

14

kitchen's serving window and enjoyed the unease of the tourists in his booth.

Rosie hustled a load of burritos from the tiny shelf of the kitchen window and called over, "Be right with you, Gabe."

"No rush."

He was halfway through his second beer when Rietman wandered back through the now filled tables and the smoke and noise, face barely visible in the dim light from the wagon-wheel chandeliers. Wager raised a hand and caught his eye.

"What'll you have?"

"Gin and tonic."

A few minutes later, Rosie, sweating now and showing her forty years, rushed past to the serving window and threw them a quick smile. "Be right with you." If she kept it up, she'd get a heart attack, Wager knew. But maybe that's what—so deep inside it was hidden even from herself—she really wanted. When she was dead, she wouldn't have to worry any more about three kids and no alimony.

"So what do you want?" Rietman wore a sport shirt and slacks, but he still moved as if he were in uniform—deliberate with the weight of authority. His face, round chin protruding almost as far as the tip of his narrow nose, was a mask before Wager's gaze.

"Tell me about Farnsworth."

"I already told Johnston and Sonnenberg about it."

"I don't want to know about the bust; I want to know about Farnsworth. What's he like, how does he deal, how'd you get to him?"

Wager waited; Rietman was halfway through his drink before he started to talk. "I was number-two man, the buyer, so most of what I know's secondhand." He finished the drink and Wager motioned for another. "Farnsworth's been up in Neder-land three, maybe four years. He comes from somewhere back East. New Jersey, I think. His old man's a doctor or lawyer or something like that. I think he went to college out here some-

15

where and maybe graduated, maybe not. A real deprived child-hood. Anyway, he's got to be the biggest of the dealers up there."

"Are they organized?"

"Not so's you can tell. It's the damnedest thing I ever heard of. The D.E.A. agent, Chandler, called them 'the big ten.' They all know each other, and if one's short, then he just calls and has a friend handle it. Otherwise they make their own deals."

"No leader? No lieutenants?"

"No. They got a thing against organizations and heavies. What did Farnsworth call it? Classical anarchism—whatever the hell that means. Anyway, it's all very loose and polite. Like they wanted to handle shit but not get their fingers smelly, if you know what I mean."

Wager ordered another round. "Who was your lead to Farnsworth?"

"Chandler. D.E.A. brought him in from Detroit."

"How'd he get solid with them?"

Rietman took another long drink. "Chandler gave them a lot of shit about being on the make as a dealer. Farnsworth really liked the guy. Chandler had a good rap and Farnsworth couldn't believe it when the bust came and there was Chandler. Hell, the whole town liked him."

"Did Chandler live up there?"

"Yeah. He rented a cabin just west of town. It took him a few months, but he got in with this guy Goldberg, who's a buddy of Farnsworth's. Then he started buying, and after a few more months he was able to call me in for a deal big enough so that only Farnsworth could cover it."

Wager sipped his beer. He'd have to come up with some-thing different; Farnsworth wouldn't buy the same package twice. "What about known associates?"

"He's shacked up with this Chicano cunt. Ramona. I think her last name's Alcalá or Alka-Seltzer or some shit like that.

16

And, let's see, there's Goldberg and Charlie Flint and Johnny Lewis and a couple others whose first names I heard, but that's all. Chandler can fill you in better than me. Why don't you talk to him?"

"I will," said Wager. "What's Farnsworth's supply?"

Rietman shook his head and finished the drink; Wager ordered another. "I don't know. But we only had to wait a day for a couple pounds, so he must either have one hell of a stash or some goddam good connections."

"Goldberg, Flint, and Lewis—they're the bagmen?"

"Naw, Gabe. Like I said, they don't have an organization. Those dudes will handle up to half a kilo. Anything bigger, they turn over to Farnsworth. That's how Chandler got to him, anyway."

"I see." He sipped at his now warm beer. "What's your story of the bust?"

Rietman cracked an ice cube between his teeth. "It was a good fucking test. I know it was a good test. But do you think that son of a bitch Sonnenberg listened to me?"

"Why?"

Two little white spots appeared at the sides of Rietman's narrow nose. "Why? Ask him—how the hell do I know! I told him I'd take a fucking lie-detector test, and the son of a bitch said it wouldn't mean a thing."

The tourists were looking nervously at Rietman. Wager motioned to Rosie for the check.

"Sonnenberg don't think the case is closed or he wouldn't be interested."

"Well, fuck him. It's closed as far as I'm concerned, and so's Sonnenberg and the whole goddam division."

"Everybody gets shit on sometime, Mark. You wait awhile and pretty soon you're on top again."

"Yeah! I'm not everybody." He set the glass down slowly. "I'll bet Sonnenberg sent you down here to try and trip me up!"

"He sent me down to find out about Farnsworth."

"I'll bet!"

Wager smiled slightly to hide his disgust. "Believe what you want to, Rietman." He stood and covered the check with a bill. "We'll see you later."

"Like hell you will."

# 2

It took Wager until noon the next day to find out that Chandler had been transferred by D.E.A. back to Detroit.

"Well, Detective Wager," said the slow voice at the other end of the line, "there wasn't no need for him to stay, now, was there? What all did you want with him?"

"Inspector Sonnenberg's looking into the Rietman thing."

"I reckon he should. Your man spilled a lot of our time and money."

He let it pass. "Do you have a number in Detroit where Chandler can be reached?"

"Hold on a minute." The voice came back: "This here's the regional office: area 313 494–9062. They can put you in touch with him."

"Thanks." He hung up and dialed the WATS operator, giving her the number. She told him she did not know how long it would take to place the call. Wager poured another cup of bitter coffee from the thermos pitcher and turned to copies of the D.E.A. files that Billy had sent over that morning. There were two Xerox pages on Farnsworth and Goldberg, but no sheets on the other names mentioned by Rietman. He called D.P.D. for any information they might have on Farnsworth, Richard Allen; Alacalá, Ramona; Goldberg, Jacob Meyer; Flint, Charles (x), a.k.a. Charlie; Lewis, John (x). The person in records said she would call back.

"All set on the truck, Gabe." He looked up to see Johnston smiling at him. "It's in your name over at the Larimer Street garage." The sergeant waited.

"That's fine, Ed."

"I—ah—had them do something special."

Wager did not like people doing something special unless he told them to do something special. "Like what?"

"You'll see. You'll like it."

He did not enjoy surprises, either. "Like what, Ed?"

"It's a little extra touch, a little more—you know—realism, like I used to do when I went under. Hey, I kind of wish it was me coming off the bench instead of you. It's been a long time."

That's all he needed: surprises from a nostalgia freak. "I'll tell you all about it."

The sergeant laughed and slapped a hand on Wager's shoulder. "There can be good times, if you follow the right game plan!"

"I'll try to do that."

"Haw! Good old Gabe!"

The telephone rang; Suzy called to him, "It's D.P.D. on some makes you requested. Are you in?"

"Yes." He picked up his receiver. "This is Detective Wager."

The brisk female voice from records said, "We have nothing on Farnsworth, Richard Allen; we do have one notation on Alcalá, Ramona, arrested in 1965 for shoplifting, guilty plea with suspended sentence. No further arrests. Goldberg, Jacob Meyer, is a negative; Flint, Charles, has three moving violations—two for speeding, one for careless driving. Last entry, June, 1974. We have four Lewis, John, Johnnys, or Jonathans. Do you know his age or place of birth?"

"Probably early to mid-twenties."

"Then we have two. One has a long record, mostly crimes against persons; the other has one entry for possession of less than an ounce."

On a hunch, he asked, "How old was Alcalá when she was arrested?"

A slight delay. "Birthdate, 21 February 1927."

That made her forty-nine—too old for his suspect. "And Flint?"

"Born 17 August 1950."

"Thanks. Could I get copies of the Flint and both Lewis jackets?"

"I'll send them over. Do you want us to query the Crime Information Center?"

"Let me get better descriptions of the suspects. I'll be back to you later."

"Yes, sir."

"Sounds like you're getting in there, Gabe. Keep driving for that goal line." Johnston gave a little punch in the air, and Wager wished the Broncos had never come to Denver.

"Has Sonnenberg contacted the Boulder sheriff's office yet?"

"I don't know—I'll find out."

"Suzy," he said as soon as the sergeant was out of sight, "I'm going over to the custodian's office. If Detroit D.E.A. calls, I'm trying to get in touch with Agent Chandler, who was just out here on special assignment. Find out how I can reach him as soon as possible."

He ducked down the pale green corridor and through the door whose buzzer rattled loudly whenever it was opened. On the tiny landing, Mrs. Gutierrez, unit security person, smiled out at him through the plexiglass window, her voice muffled by the baffles mounted over the window's speakhole. "Have a good day, Detective Wager."

He waved at her smile and graying hair and thumped down the worn stairs before Johnston could call him back for another pep talk.

The D.P.D. custodian's office was in the rear of the Main Police Headquarters, a concrete building just south of the convention complex. It stood foursquare, four stories, and was crowned with a large red-and-white antenna; the new justice complex, which should have been completed by now, was several blocks away, a cluster of raw concrete pillars sprouting reinforcing rods. Meanwhile, D.P.D. made do—as usual—with overcrowded space and a parking lot so jammed with official vehicles and unmarked cars that he had to wait ten minutes before a patrol car bounced through the gate and gave him space to park.

The property locker of the custodian's office was run by a civilian Caucasian female, mid-twenties, brown eyes, dark hair longer than allowed for non-civilian personnel and serving to draw attention to a face that was passably good-looking. The identification card clipped above a nice full breast read, Miller, Elizabeth M. Wager rested his own I.D. on the shelf of the half-door.

"I'd like to see the custodial reports on D.E.A.-6, file number 31942, Farnsworth, Richard Allen."

"Yes, sir. Would you sign a check-out form please?"

Wager looked at the small pad of yellow mimeographed paper. "This is something new?"

"Yes, sir. For better security." She bent to pull the file from a cabinet and Wager admired her legs: slender and firm and straight. With a little better face, she really would be nice. She laid the file on the shelf and watched him with eyes made larger and darker by a faint touch of eye shadow.

22

He found an almost quiet corner of the busy corridor and leaned against a wall to study the laboratory analysis and custody sheet. The suspect material had been checked into property with a request for analysis at 10:38 P.M. by Rietman, initialed by the night clerk, W.G., then checked out again at 1:07 P.M. the following day by A.D. That would be Archie Douglas, the chief technician at the lab. At 4:13 P.M. it was checked back in by E.M., with a copy of the lab report: 96% lactose, 3% inert matter, 1% cocaine trace. That was all—traces don't make cases. Out of habit, he copied the facts into his small wire-bound notebook and took the papers back to the property room.

"Thanks, miss."

She dropped the manila folder back into the drawer.

"Do you know who 'W.G.'s is? He was on duty last Thursday night."

"Wilma Green. She's a uniformed officer."

"Thanks again." Wager filled in the blank spot on his page and smiled good-bye to Miss Miller. She did not smile back; to hell with her.

In his car, Wager radioed Suzy: "Two-one-six?"

"This is two-one-six."

"Two-one-two. Anything yet from Detroit?"

"Negative."

"Ten-four."

Hansen's call numbers were two-one-four; Wager radioed them, and the detective's voice came back quickly in reply, "Go ahead, two-one-two."

"Are you in District 1?"

"Yeah, a few blocks from unit headquarters on Colfax."

"Meet me there in ten."

It was back to headquarters whether he wanted it or not. Johnston was waiting. "Hey, Gabe! Here's the name of your liaison in Boulder—Sergeant Paul Mayhew. He's with the sheriff's office, and the inspector says he's first string."

23

"Mayhew in the S.O. Thanks, Ed."

Ed gave the little punch in the air. "We'll get the bastards, Gabe."

Hansen was sitting at his desk; Wager nodded to him. "Did Johnston tell you that you'll be taking some of my cases?"

Hansen's eyes rounded. "No. You got a special?"

"Yes. Here's what I've been doing." He pulled a small deck of contact cards from his own desk and sat on the corner of Hansen's. "There's a buy and bust tomorrow afternoon in Cheeseman Park. Pinetti's the contact man—he's on loan from Crimes Against Persons. Give him a call and let him know you'll be handling the surveillance. One of my C.I.s says he's onto something big; he's always onto something big, but it has to be listened to just in case. That's Doc. Fat Willy is setting up a dude in the Points. I'll call them now and say you're covering for me. Let's see. . . . This one may build into something. It's a lead into Pueblo, and the C.I. thinks it's tied into Mexican heroin. He's just on the edge of the action, but the next month or two should tell. The rest of these"—he tapped the cards—"I'll give to Ashcroft."

Hansen finished making a few notes and looked up, pulling at the tip of his ragged brown mustache. "How long are you gone for?"

"No idea."

"Where to?"

"The Western Slope." If Hansen or anybody else had a need to know more, Ed would tell them. If not, he wouldn't.

"Jesus. I'll bet it's Aspen. That place is dope city any more."

"The whole Western Slope is unreal."

"Yeah. Say, have you seen Reitman?"

"Yesterday."

"I hear he's pretty sore."

Wager grunted, *"Me cae gordo."*

"Boy, I'd be sore, too, if it was me. He claims he ran a good test."

"That's what he says. But it's happened to other people, too."

"Still, it sure is too bad." Hansen's line buzzed.

Wager turned to his own desk to leaf through the little book of coded numbers for his C.I.s. The first one he dialed rang twice before a wheezing, sleepy voice said, "Uh-huh"

"It's Gabe, Willy. I'm going out of town for a while. You'll be working with Hansen. You know him?"

"No, I don't know him, man. And I don't dig this shit of you handing me around like I was a motherfucking dog or something. Why don't you just put my fucking name on the bulletin board down there or something?"

"It can't be helped, Willy."

"Say, man, maybe Fat Willy can help it."

"Hansen's got all the bread now, Fat Man. If you want some, work with him. If not, wait'll I get back. It's up to you."

In the pause, Wager heard the black's slow, fleshy breath. "How long you gonna be out of town?"

"A couple months. Maybe more."

"Jesus Hebrew Christ! I been working with you for three years and now you pull shit like this. You pass me around like that, and people gonna find out who I am. You don't think nothing of leaving me hanging by the balls, do you?"

Wager didn't. "It's part of the job."

"Yeah! Well, maybe me and this Hansen dude will get along. Maybe I won't want no more of your shit when you get back!"

"Willy, I'll bring you a little present."

"Shee-it!" The line went dead. Wager pictured the huge black figure wheezing and grunting curses as he always did when his routine was changed and the cold breeze of fear went across hs sweating back. But he would work for Hansen, Wager knew. The big man was always hungry. And he would work for Wager later, for as long as Wager needed him—or as long as he lasted.

The second number was answered by a woman whose voice Wager did not recognize. "Is Doc there?"

The male voice came on quickly, "Who's it?"

"It's Gabe. You got another old lady already?"

"Hey, man, yeah! Really far out! It's about time you called —hey, I'm really onto it big this time."

"Right, Doc. Listen . . ."

The high-pitched voice cut in, "We can get it by the pound, man—I mean really heavy!"

"Listen, Doc—I'm going out of town for a while. You'll be working with Detective Hansen."

"Who? What's his first name?"

"Hansen. Roger Hansen."

"I got it. It's really big, man. Too bad you're gonna miss it."

"Right, I'm all broken up, too. But listen, now, don't give Hansen bad hype."

"Naw, naw. I wouldn't shit him any more than I would you. Tell him to call me as soon as he can, you hear?"

"Sure will, Doc." Wager hung up and jotted both numbers on a page torn from the small notebook. He slipped it on Hansen's desk. "Willy's not happy about the switch, but he'll come around. Doc wants you to call him right away, but don't waste too much time on him."

"He's not reliable?"

"Sometimes he comes up with something solid, but he's not consistent. Still, make him think you're with him. He really eats that crap up."

"I know the type," said Hansen. The younger detective fingered the page with the numbers. "You really think Rietman just fucked up?"

Wager stared at him, "What?"

"Well, Rietman could of—well—if he was the type, I mean, he could of maybe switched."

Wager looked at Hansen as if seeing him for the first time:

light brown hair long and curling down his neck and over the tops of his ears, eyes gray against the tanned face, mustache also slightly curly and turned down below the corners of his mouth to end in tiny clumps of wild hair. "Reitman's a cop."

"Well I was just . . ."

"If you got evidence, you take it to Sonnenberg or the Staff Investigation Bureau. If you don't, you shut up. *¿Comprendes tú?*"

"It happens, Wager!" Hansen's tan darkened. "Rietman may be a cop, but it does happen sometimes."

That was true. But you didn't go around saying something like that, especially about anyone in your own unit. A cop is a cop until it's *proved* he's not. "Rietman's a cop," he said again, and turned back to his desk.

The Detroit call came through at 3:27, and Wager was given three telephone numbers where Agent Chandler might be found. "Say," the Detroit D.E.A. man finished, "what happened out there, anyway?"

"That's what I'm trying to find out," said Wager, and hung up. The first number just rang; the second was answered by a woman, and from the way she said hello Wager pictured a housewife who did not want her husband's business invading his home life. "Can I talk to Agent Chandler, please?"

"Well, he's asleep right now."

"This is Detective Wager in Denver, Colorado, and it's very important, ma'am."

"Well, just a minute, then."

A groggy voice eventually sighed, "Chandler."

"This is Detective Wager with the Denver Police Department. I'd like some more information on the Farnsworth case."

"Jesus—Farnsworth! You people out there have my reports."

"Just a few things your report didn't cover that might help us out."

"Yeah—you people need all the help you can get. All right."
The voice pulled away from the mouthpiece to say, "Get me some coffee, honey."

Wager poured himself another cup from the thermos. "Can you give me the vitals on Ramona Alcalá—if that's her name —Charles Flint, and John Lewis?"

"It's Alcalá; around twenty-three, five two, a hundred and ten, dark hair and eyes. She's a greaser. She's got a big birthmark near her elbow on her right arm. Charlie Flint's a little older, white, around twenty-seven, five ten, one sixty-five; his face is full of red beard. I didn't see any scars or marks. He's an art freak—wants to get enough bread to set up a gallery in Aspen or Taos or wherever. He's full of sh—uh—hot air, always using fancy words. Lewis's alias is Jo-Jo. He's kind of weird; I had my eye on him to flip him. He still might if he's squeezed, but you got to watch him and he's not really one of the top operators, anyway. He makes it as a middler. Penny-a-pound stuff. He's white, about twenty-one, five eleven, a hundred and forty. Light-brown Afro-style hair, hazel eyes. He tries to be a political activist. That's the thing with a lot of them now—support radical movements, start a commune, that kind of crap."

Wager finished his line of unorthodox shorthand in the little notebook. "Any other known associates?"

"The whole damn town."

"They're *all* dealing?"

"Well, I tell you. Out of a population of maybe five hundred, I could touch a hundred small-timers. But most of them were just divvying their own stash. The real core is about ten people, and Farnsworth seems to be the main source for all of them."

"Does he run it himself?"

"He's made some trips to Colombia and Venezuela, him and Ramona. But I think he's got his own mules now who bring it in through California and sometimes Canada. That's all guesswork, though, and he trades a lot of coke for other stuff."

28

"What about the other four hundred?"

"They're either rednecks or clean freaks, and they hate each other's guts. We almost had us a vigilante war between the straights and the hips. I used to think Detroit was the nut house of the universe, but you people have some real winners out there."

Wager spoke as softly as possible but could not keep the heavier accent from his voice. "It's the altitude—thin air and x-rays. Farnsworth's operation—maybe you can tell me something about it?"

"Boy, it's a joy to behold. That son of a gun just sits up there and makes money hand over fist. I could have spent ten kilo a day if I had it, and Farns would have gotten a cut of it all. Coke, acid, grass, hash, magic mushroom—you name it, Farns can get it. They've got a kind of co-op; the big ten cover for each other and so far everybody's happy. All the top ones, anyway. Farnsworth's not laying it all over everybody that he's the heavy. Honor among pushers, you know."

"Never heard of it."

"Naw, me neither until I saw that operation. But it's true. If one's short, he'll steer you to somebody who can handle it. Maybe they have a set of books to keep it all straight; maybe they just remember. I don't know. I think they're just making so much that they can afford not to be greedy."

"Any places they're known to frequent?"

"There aren't many places up there. The Timber Line Tavern's where everybody hangs out. It's in colorful downtown Nederland—you can't miss it. If you did, you'd end up in the lake."

"Do buyers come up there?"

"A lot do. That was my cover. Like I say, there's maybe a hundred small dealers that get supplied by the big ten. Most of them go to Boulder, Denver, Fort Collins, and all over Jefferson County. Up to Estes Park, too, but there's a lot of competition up there from people who bring their own stuff

from both coasts and up from Texas. I couldn't check it all out
—hell, I had ten primary targets and it was all I could do to
handle them."

"Can you give me a list?"

"Look, why don't I just send you a copy of what I've got?
I don't have all my notes at home."

"Just one more question. What happened on the bust?"

"That's a good question—Rietman ran the reagent test and
gave the signal for the bust. Neither one of them were worth
a damn."

"Did you watch him test it?"

"No, I was in Farnsworth's car with the front money. Rietman and Goldberg were in the government vehicle. That was
the deal: I went with the money, Goldberg went with the dope
until it was checked out. Then we were supposed to leave the
money and the dope and walk back to our cars and drive away.
You know how an exchange is set up."

"You and Rietman were in separate cars—him and Goldberg, you and Farnsworth?" Maybe the question wasn't his to
ask, but he was a cop. And despite what he had said to Hansen,
an ugly thought began to lie restless in his mind.

"Yeah."

"What happened then?"

"Well, we told them it was a bust and covered them, and
neither one tried anything. They were cool—they knew when
they were took. Rietman had the radio and called in the surveillance, and then we all went to Denver."

"Who drove what?"

"I drove Farnsworth's car and Rietman drove his."

"His was the government vehicle?"

"Yeah."

"Alone?"

"Yeah, the suspects were put in custody of the surveillance
team—they had more people to secure the prisoners—and they
transported them to headquarters."

"Did you all go straight to D.P.D?"

Chandler gave a short laugh. "Yeah, it looked like a god-darned parade."

"What time did you get there?"

"Oh, between ten and eleven. An hour or so after the meet."

"What about the dope?"

"What about it?"

"Did it stay in Rietman's possession or go with you or with the surveillance team?"

The long-distance line hummed and clicked faintly. Finally Chandler said, "Rietman kept it."

And logged it into the police locker at—Wager looked in his notebook—10:38 P.M.

"Say, Wager, are you with D.P.D.'s internal security?"

"No, I'm just trying to get some facts straight, Chandler."

A guarded note had come into Chandler's voice; it wasn't worry—he was just putting distance between himself and trouble. "Well, I wasn't with Rietman that much, you know, but he seemed O.K. And God knows it wouldn't be the first time somebody ran a bad color test."

"I'm glad to hear that. And I'd appreciate having copies of your documents on the case as soon as possible," Wager said.

"O.K.—ah, I'll send them to our office in Denver and you can pick them up there." That would be a little more distance for Chandler.

"Fine. Send them in care of Agent Billington."

"Billington. Will do."

Wager sat staring at the cradled receiver, not really hearing the bustle and jingle of the warren of offices around him. Outside, west of the sprawling city and beyond the occasional skeleton of new offices or apartment towers that were beginning to erupt here and there, loomed the mountains. In the late-afternoon light their colors were blurred by the fall of shadows, the tan and green and white of timberline and snow-field turning into ridges of dusty gray lifting one behind the other. It was summer in the hills and he was missing it again. In the hills, he could be alone and washed clean by white sunlight and that cold high-altitude wind. Maybe. Farnsworth was in the hills, too. The Farnsworths were everywhere now. And Wager wasn't in the hills. He was in an ugly avocado-green office sitting at a gray metal desk and vaguely hearing Hansen's voice behind him setting up a meet with Doc.

He poured another cup of coffee and leafed through the small notebook. Rietman could have done it—run the test, called for the bust, loaded up the suspects, and then just reached under the front seat of his own car and pulled out a package of lactose and wrapped it in the original cover. He'd know beforehand how much lactose he'd need; he wouldn't have known how easy the switch would be. But he could gamble on that. For a quick profit of anywhere between $85,000 in bulk and a million in street sales for the two and a half pounds, Rietman could have gambled. And that would sure cushion the hassle of running a bad test. Except that Rietman claimed it was a good test. Still, what else could he claim? And how else could he act? And what the hell did he, Wager, do now?

His coffee was cold; he poured it back into the thermos and wandered without seeing back through the labyrinth of partitions and jutting desks to the coffee machine for a hot refill. It could have been an honest mistake. Officers had made mistakes before, especially on their first big buy like this one, when they tended to see what they wanted to see. Maybe the reagent kit hadn't been cleaned—the lab report showed a trace of cocaine; maybe Rietman really did see some color and thought the suspect material had been cut to, say, 30 percent from the original 70, and that explained the color's thinness. Because Rietman was a cop, god damn it, and cops didn't—shouldn't —do things like that! And you didn't go walking into Sonnenberg's office with an accusation against a fellow officer unless you had a hell of a lot more than guesswork or even circumstantial evidence. You didn't even whisper those things or bring them up like Hansen did, because that eroded the vital trust an officer had to have in his companions.

But it was possible.

And Wager knew how alone and unknown, finally, every cop was.

Johnston called to him from his cubicle, "Have you picked up the truck yet, Gabe?"

Wager broke his stare at Rietman's empty desk. "I haven't had a chance, Ed."

"Oh." A faint tinge of disappointment. "Well, I have some expense money for you. Do you want to sign for it now?"

"Sure." In Johnston's little office, he counted the worn twenties and tens and filled in the blank on the form for receipt of official funds.

"You think two thousand will get you started?"

"Sure. I don't want to come on too strong at first."

"Something wrong?"

"Why?"

"You seem down."

"No. I'm just thinking."

"Well . . . go get 'em."

"Right, Ed." He folded the money and shoved it into the pocket of his sport coat; then he sat again at his desk without really doing anything. Finally, he mumbled *"Mierda"* and pushed away from the yellow manila folders that seemed to be looking back at him. "Suzy, I'm going over to the garage."

"Do you have any calls pending?"

"Nothing."

The Larimer Street garage was almost empty this late in the afternoon; on the busy street the homebound traffic roared past in a river of gray-brown exhaust and treeless heat. Inside the large building the sun's weight was lifted by shadow. In the rear, from a long workbench dark with oil and dirt, a radio pushed thin music into the garage's silence. Wager wandered around until he found a corner of the building partitioned off by bare plywood sheets. The officer on duty was reading *Sports Afield.*

"I'm Detective Wager from the O.C.D. Sergeant Johnston said you people had a truck for me."

"Wager?" The blue-uniformed figure stood and lifted down a set of keys from a row of small hooks. "Yes, sir, Detective Wager. Would you like to look it over?"

"Yes."

The officer led him out a side door and into the compound behind the building. "I think the boys done a real good job."

Wager looked at the light blue truck gleaming with its new paint. "You didn't rig it for a radio pack, did you?"

"No, sir. And we put in a rifle rack, as well as the special paint job."

"What special paint job?"

"Right here! Didn't you want this? Sergeant Johnston said to put it on." He pointed at the cab's window ledge; in red, orange, and white outline were scrolled tiny flowers arcing into a small but fancy "G.V." Gabriel Villanueva.

Wager almost smiled; it was a good touch. Sometimes Ed really did have a good idea. "It looks real fine," he said.

# 3

The shortest way to Nederland was up the Boulder turnpike and then Boulder canyon. Wager took the longest way to delay what he would have to do to himself: I-70 to Golden, past the drab concrete boxes of the Coors factory, and halfway up the narrow twists and tunnels of Clear Creek to the Central City turnoff. Then right along the Peak-to-Peak Highway, up and down the long slopes of pine-covered Front Range, gazing at the snowy raggedness of the Continental Divide just to the west. Even in midweek, the summer highway was clogged with out-of-state drivers—the pumpkin-colored plates of New York, the various blues of California, red and white from Nebraska, black and white from Texas. All driving like flatlanders, slowing to a crawl on the easy turns, speeding up on the straight so no one could pass. But Wager was in no rush. He poked behind the tourists and took time to gaze at the empty and rotting mine hoppers riding eruptions of rock and bleached sand; to look again at the mounds of gravel and stone sumped from the creek beds and only now, a century later, beginning to sprout tufts of grass and anemic struggling saplings. All that waste, all that wealth—the waste remaining, the wealth gone decades ago to Eastern banks, to European owners, and now to out-of-state corporations whose modern angular initials hinted at some new threatening mechanism. Now the Easterners, the corporations, wanted to do it again for coal and oil shale: rip open the land and take the wealth, leave the state poorer than when they came, leave their dumped garbage to be cleaned up by people like Wager who were paid to wipe up other people's messes. They even took the profits of cattle and agriculture and recreation—gone from the state to absentee owners who paid minimum tax on farmland and on tar-paper shacks used only in the summer. The state's residents were cattle for a new kind of slaughter, dogs for a new kind of whipping. If he were younger and had not seen so much, if he had been born in a later time and had been given different answers or no answers at all, he might have joined his nephews in their marches, blaming classes and races and economics and "ism"s. But while he could understand their anger, he could not understand their answers. To Wager, the fault lay in something more permanent and widespread, something he had seen enough of to get sick of: human nature. And for him there were no big answers —people were going to rip the earth and each other, and his job was to stop those who ripped more than the law allowed. That was the answer he had to be satisfied with; and if sometimes—like now—he felt that he was one of a bunch of giggling kids so intent on their own fun and games that they never raised their eyes to their fall-through-dark emptiness, he could only ask again: What else was there? This was what he was given, and the only value lay in doing it well.

He studied his face once more in the tiny rectangle of the rear-view mirror. The past week had been slow, but necessarily so; a man's beard only grew so fast. The goatee was thin but noticeable and the sideburns sprouted down his jaws in feathers of dark hair. With sunglasses and the flat hat, he looked different enough from Detective Wager of the O.C.D. to pass for Gabe Villanueva, new kid on the block. He hoped. There was always the possibility that it would not work, that his cover—like him—would be blown away. The small civilian pistol, a Bauer .25 caliber, shoved into the back of his Levis prodded him into that thought. But to Wager's mind, most dealers wanted nothing to do with wiping a narc. Without a resistance charge, the odds favored them in court. He shook his head slightly. The criminal wasn't on trial any more, but police procedure was; the guilt or innocence of a suspect didn't count, but the technology of presenting evidence did. And there were a hell of a lot more ways a cop could play the game wrong than right. Ask Rietman.

The truck bumped stiffly over a frost heave in the asphalt road, rocking the straw cowboy hat hanging on one prong of the rifle rack. The other prong sprouted the half-used roll of toilet paper in a shade of delicate pink. Truck, beard, and story—all of it had to be convincing. He had to wrap it around him like a blanket, so that none of him—not even his eyes, which might leak what he thought—could be seen. He had to lose himself, and he didn't like it.

The effect had already been seen earlier in the week with Billy, when he brought over the papers that Chandler had sent to the Denver D.E.A. office. Billington stood at a new distance from what he saw, and he tried to overcome his embarrassment with a joke. "Gawd, Gabe! I better have the immigration people check your birth certificate."

Wager saw nothing funny in it; the week was a waste of time and his new beard itched. "Did you get Chandler's stuff?"

"Yeah, here. Jesus, you ought to get busted for being ugly in public."

"Have a beer—I'd like to look these over."

Billy wandered toward the kitchen; Wager spread the slick photo paper on the small glass table between the two sling chairs. There were three sheets of Xeroxed contact cards, a list of the big ten with a short description: Farnsworth and Alcalá, Goldberg, Flint, and Lewis were at the top. Then came: Crowley, Theodore, a.k.a. Ted, T.D., white male, mid-twenties, dark hair, heavy build, 6'2"; Baca, Manuel, a.k.a. Manny, "The Man," Chicano male, early twenties, dark hair and eyes, slender, 5'10"; Kettler, William, a.k.a. Bill, white male, late teens, brown hair and eyes, 5'10", around 200 pounds; Dodd, Gary, a.k.a. "Bones," white male, twenty-two, dark hair, blue eyes, 6'1", 140 pounds; and, also believed to be a member of the big ten, Cocky Gallegos, Chicano male, late twenties, dark hair and eyes, 5'8", about 175 pounds.

"Nothing more than this on Farnsworth? What about the arrest record?"

"We had to destroy his file—it wasn't a valid arrest."

Wager grunted and started back through the names, poised for any gentle tug at his memory.

"Hey, when are you gonna give this place some life?" Billy gazed at the blank walls and wide expanses of empty carpet. "Since you and Lorraine split up, you've been living in a goddam barracks."

Wager looked around; the apartment's living room had the two canvas chairs and glass table, a portable TV on its stand, a small table for the telephone. "It looks O.K. to me."

"Didn't you have some pictures on the walls?"

"They were Lorraine's. She took them."

"That card table's all you got in the kitchen?"

"I like it."

Billy shook his head and drained the beer can; its bottom gave a tinny clink. "Well, it seems kind of . . . alienated . . . to me."

"I don't spend much time here." Billy was one of the growing number of officers who had a college degree—psychology. Usually he kept quiet about it, but every now and then Wager could hear some textbook language. Still, it hadn't spoiled him for police work as it had spoiled so many others; Billy was his ex-partner, and he was a good man. Besides, now that he noticed them, the walls did seem to be empty and waiting. Billy might have a point. "Maybe I'll hang up one of those big color photographs—the Maroon Belles. How would that look over there?"

Billy glanced at him and then quickly away. "I think that would be fine."

Wager turned back to the papers and finished copying the information into his small notebook; then he telephoned D.P.D. "This is Detective Wager. I need a crime information check on these names and descriptions." He read the list and waited while the woman read it back.

"Do you have a driver's license number or other form of identification for any of these, Detective Wager?" she asked.

He would have told her if he did. "No."

"It may take a while without a driver's license or a Social Security number."

He knew that, too. "Yes."

"Do you want them run through C.B.I. also?"

"Complete check: C.I.C. and C.B.I. Call me at 837–9305 when they clear."

"Yes, sir. Will do." The voice clicked off like a recording.

Billy stood looking across the apartment's little stucco balcony at the ranges of peaks lifting west of Denver. "Have you ever heard of Larry Ginsdale or Oscar Pitkin?"

Wager couldn't place the names. "No. Are you working on them?"

"Jesus, no! We got enough going on already."

But Billy wasn't the type to scratch unless something itched. "Then what's special about them?" Wager asked.

"We picked up on those names a few months back—just

little crap at first. You know, a cut ounce here and there. They're heads from California, but they haven't been dealing heavy, so we didn't waste time on them."

"And now?"

"Now the word on the street is that they can deliver as much cocaine as anybody wants, and at anywhere from five to ten below the market price."

"They found a sweet contact."

"No lie. But the thing is they've been small-time up till now. Hell, they were retailers and middlers in California. They come here, and in a few months they start wholesaling. Now, just a couple months more, and they're supposed to have one of the world's biggest stashes."

"You believe they're tied in with Farnsworth?"

"I thought you'd never ask! They don't have any links with any of the dealers we know up in Aspen, and they've got to be getting it somewhere."

Wager nodded. To a civilian, two officers playing "Do you know?" might sound like a lot of wasted time. But that was the way information was traded, and information led to convictions. Too bad it was so seldom shared between D.E.A. agents and the local units. Or even between officers in neighboring outfits. Jealousy about credit for a bust, jurisdictional disputes, even suspicion and security worries kept the agencies apart; and Colorado was one of the few states that had no statewide narcotics unit. As if a dealer's routes of supply and selling were limited to only one township or even a county! He and Billy were lucky that they had been partners; they had built trust in each other. You had to trust the guy who covered your back. Wager really hoped that D.E.A. would keep Billy in the region. "I'll let you know what I hear." He jotted the names on a blank page of his notebook and put Billy's initials after them.

Billington tossed the beer can into the paper bag that served as a kitchen wastebasket. "Anything else you need from Chandler? I'll get it for you if you do."

40

"Not yet. If I think of something, I'll yell."

"Well, I got to Serve and Protect—you take it easy up in the hills."

"It'll be a vacation."

Half an hour after Billy left, Wager's telephone rang; the police person in criminal identification had the read-out. "It's negative on the following names." Wager wondered if her face was as stiff as her voice. "Crowley, Dodd, Gallegos. Baca was arrested by the F.B.I. in June, 1974, on a bombing charge in Fort Collins, Colorado. No conviction. Arrested by D.P.D. in March, 1975, for possession of less than an ounce of marijuana; received suspended sentence in June, 1975. Current address, Route 1, Nederland, Colorado. Kettler has one arrest in Boston, Massachusetts, in September, 1973; pleaded guilty in juvenile court to possession, received suspended sentence. Current address is unknown."

Wager thanked the voice and jotted the facts on the copy paper while they still sounded in his ear. Tougher and tougher: not only a small community and a suspect already frightened from almost being burned, but a bunch of people without records who, if arrested, wouldn't give him much of a handle; their lawyers would damn well know how light the sentence on a first conviction would be. Still, out of all these people, it would only take one to land Farnsworth. Maybe "Manny the Man" Baca: bombs, fights, dope; he might be one of the *hermanos*, and that would offer an angle. Both Sonnenberg and Chandler had mentioned radical types. Wager turned back through the notebook pages to the telephone conversation with Chandler; he had mentioned another possibility: Jo-Jo Lewis. A little weird, Chandler had called him. Those were the ones that were dynamite; those were the ones you had to watch even on a routine traffic stop. But hell, as far as Wager was concerned, they were all a little weird. Some were just weirder than others.

Sergeant Johnston called the next morning to say that the

jackets on Flint and Lewis had arrived from D.P.D. "You coming down for them?"

"Just put them on my desk, Ed. I'll be down later this afternoon." He felt like a snake growing a new skin, and did not want people to see him shedding; he could already hear Mrs. Gutierrez's voice rise through the little plexiglass window: "My, Detective Wager, you do look different!" After five o'clock he could get in and not be seen.

"Did you, ah, pick up the truck, Gabe?"

The initials painted on the door! "Yes—that was a good idea you had."

The sergeant's voice smiled. "Yeah, I thought so, too. I remember I saw a lot of trucks painted like that down in Galveston."

"You're right, Ed. It was a good touch."

"Yeah. Well, check in before you go up there; we might have some last-minute information for you."

"I will, Ed."

A long afternoon passed before he headed for the office in that lull of traffic that comes just after the rush hour and just before the evening bustle. Letting himself in with his passkey, he closed the metal door quickly to shut off the buzzer that sounded twice as raucous in the empty rooms. From somewhere behind one of the pale green partitions and across the silent desks and typewriters, floated the country and Western music of the duty watch's radio. A telephone rang once, twice; the duty watch's voice murmured into the receiver. Wager swung into the O.C.D. cubicle, surprised to see Hansen busily scratching on forms with a ballpoint pen.

"You collecting overtime, Rog?"

The younger man looked startled, "Holy Moly! I didn't recognize you for a minute, Gabe." He fingered his own chin. "You look like goddam Pancho Villa or somebody. Say, are you on assignment? That Western Slope thing?"

"Yes." He picked up the Flint and two Lewis folders from

his "in" box where Johnston had left them. "Are things busy?"

"Your C.I. Doc set up a deal on grass. He claims he knows some dude who can get it by the ton. We're meeting in a little while."

"Don't let him pull you through the grease."

Hansen shrugged. "It's all got to be looked at. This Western Slope thing you're on, is it really big?"

Wager said no. He didn't like such questions, even from a fellow officer, unless they dealt with specific suspects. General questions sounded plain nosy, and a cop should have enough work of his own without sticking his nose into someone else's. Leafing through the slim folders, he began making notes. Charles James Flint. Traffic citations only; Wager took down his driver's license number and address: 103 Main Street, Nederland. An art freak, Chandler had said. What the hell did Wager know about art? The Lewis jackets were criminal entries; the closed faces gazed out of the small photographs with their inch markers down the left side. The single entry—possession of less than an ounce—was the John Lewis he wanted: 5'10", brown hair, slender build. Route 1, Nederland. The face in the color photograph was too young to have a beard, though a scattering of hairs tried to pass for one among the pimply blotches on his jaw.

"Oh, Gabe?"

He looked up.

"Fat Willy is really pissed at being handed over to me."

"Didn't he show up for the Five Points meet?"

"Yeah, but he sure didn't like it."

"Tough. Just keep him on a tight leash—he always needs money."

"Will do."

Suzy had left a few messages for him. Near the top of the pile was a note from Sonnenberg: "Gabe—Boulder S.O. wants you to check in with the Nederland marshal's office when you get there. Jurisdiction. W.S." Jesus Christ—maybe he should check in with Farnsworth, too. Two C.I.s left calls; Wager noted "Give to Ashcroft" on the slips of paper and stuck them under the roller of Suzy's typewriter. Ashcroft could use some overtime money, too, if he ever got a vacation to spend it. The rest of the paperwork was routine crap and could wait until he came back. He was always a little cynically surprised at how quickly much of the paperwork lost its importance when it sat for a week or so. Near the bottom of the pile was a message from Colorado Springs: "Vital you call back," with a number. It was two days old. He dialed; on the fifth ring, a man's hoarse whisper said "Hello?"

"This is Gabe."

A moment of silence. "No, there ain't no Fred here." Someone was with him; he would call back when he could. Wager said the office number and hung up. Hansen finished his scribbling and logged out on the acetate name chart under the column headed "On Pager." Gabe waved a hand good night and looked up the Nederland marshal's office in the law enforcement directory.

"Is this Marshal Farrell?"

"It is." He sounded like a young man trying to make his voice lower, possibly a patrolman with just a year or two of experience who could be hired cheaply. Maybe even a civilian who always wanted to be a cop and could be hired even cheaper.

"This is Detective Wager down in Denver with the O.C.D. Marshal Farrell, we've got a case that's going to involve some undercover work in your township. We'll have at least one man working up there for a while."

"Wager, is it? What's the nature of the case, Detective Wager?"

"Narcotics."

"Yep, I figured. We do have problems along them lines, that's for sure. You want to tell me your man's name?"

44

"We don't know yet, Marshal. He'll be coming in from out of state."

"How about D.E.A.? They gonna come back, too?"

"I don't know."

"How long's your operation going to last?"

"Well, you know how these things go. It might be a while."

"Yep. Well, you tell him to get in touch with me if he needs my help. I'm damned glad to know somebody's coming up here."

Wager thought the relief sounded genuine. "I'll do that, Marshal."

He scrawled a quick message on the bottom of Sonnenberg's note and put it in the inspector's box: "Done, Wager." Then he headed for the firing range; it would be empty at this time of day, and the stifling inaction of the long week made him hungry for the sound and smell of gunpowder. Strange how popping a few caps was almost as good as exercise for blowing the cobwebs out of the system; it was satisfying to feel the butt of the pistol thump against his arm, to see the shreds of cardboard spray out behind the target right where the notch and blade of the sight had rested. Very simple, very direct, very satisfying. Tomorrow, he would make the first run up to Nederland.

He straightened the rear-view mirror and set the leather hat square over his eyes, tugged the turquoise-and-silver necklace a bit higher so it could be seen through his collar. Everything except the patchouli oil, and he'd be damned or dead before he splashed that crap in his armpits.

The road curved past an azure pond of water that set off the white and gray of the ragged Indian Peaks; then a series of switchbacks led through heavy pine forests down to the wide, shallow valley of the townsite. A few midday clouds were gathering into what would become the thunderstorms of late afternoon, while above them the sky held the cold, almost brittle blue of high altitude. It was all too lovely, too clean. Somehow it made the reason for his trip all the more obscene.

# 4

Wager went up to Nederland three or four times the first week to drink a slow beer at each of the town's few bars, to be seen strolling like a tourist from the sagging old grocery store to the glass-and-plastic hamburger stand, to the log-fronted hardware store and the brick post office, where a line of chatting hippies stood waiting for food stamps. When a week had passed with only a cautious nod from a bartender or two, Gabe visited the Indian Peaks Gallery.

"May I help you?" Behind a small desk in the entry alcove of the old frame house sat Charles Flint, red hair and beard fanning out to surround his pale blue eyes. Wager recognized him from the D.P.D. jacket, though he looked a little heavier than his description noted.

"I'm looking for some nice photographs." He tried to sound comfortable as he gazed at lavender macramé hangings, square canvases of glossy colors running over each other, a series of rusty gears welded roughly together and priced at $350.

"Anything in particular?"

"Well, mountains and trees."

Flint's whiskers moved in what Wager thought was a smile. "You might find something of interest in that room." He pointed at what used to be the parlor of the narrow house. "Please take a look around; if you need anything, just ask."

"Thanks." He made himself grin back.

Wager did have mountains and trees in mind: that large photograph of the Maroon Belles, the one with the lake in the foreground framed by spruce and golden aspens, the three triangular peaks dark red against a clear blue sky. It was a familiar picture, one he always liked. Some versions that he had seen even had small flowers painted into the grass of the fore-ground. That made it even prettier.

Instead, he found the walls of the empty room hung with small pictures in wide paper frames: a single daisy against an out-of-focus background that could have been mountains; a naked leg curled beside a rough boulder; a close-up of a weath-ered barn door. Wager knew what he liked, and this wasn't it; a picture should show something and not just a piece of it. He guessed that the guy who took it was stoned or maybe you had to be stoned to like it. Slowly walking through the rooms, he let Flint hear the gentle creak of the old floorboards, the meditative scuff of a slow-moving heel. And Wager heard something, too: in his mind he heard his father's laughing voice when facing some puzzlement from the Hispano world: *"Estoy como perro en barrio ajeno."* Though Wager's smile had a different twist from his father's, he also felt that way: like a dog in a foreign neighborhood. After a long twenty minutes, he wandered back to Flint's desk.

"Find something?" The red-haired face looked up from a sheaf of papers; he was only a struggling businessman trying to make an honest buck.

"Well . . . those are pretty good, all right. But I kind of wanted a big picture. A lot of mountains with maybe a lake in front. You've seen that one of the Maroon Belles?"

In the still air, Flint's fingernails rasped on the creased neck beneath his beard. "Who hasn't?" He shook his head. "Perhaps you can try the gallery down the block. Or maybe Woolworth's in Denver—the basement store. They might have the selection you're looking for."

"Yeah—I live in Denver. I just wanted something that would bring the mountains into my living room." He made himself smile again.

"We do have some selections that aren't displayed—let me get them."

He watched Flint unfold from the desk chair and disappear into another small room; drawers slid open and shut, and a few minutes later he came back with an armful of cardboard frames.

"I tend to specialize in expressionistic photography; however, some of these are exceptionally good and perhaps you'll find just the mood you want." He set them on a low table beneath a stringy potted plant, hanging from the ceiling in a woven net, priced at $25. "Now here's one that captures the isolated individual against the mystery of darkness." He held up a photograph that, if you looked closely, was in color: a single dead tree standing whitely against the almost black of solid forest. It had neither water nor sky.

"That's mighty nice, all right."

"Here's one that reflects the living light of mountain water." A blurred tumble of white streaks scarred across sun-glinted water that was slightly out of focus.

"Um-hum," said Wager.

"And this is one of my favorites, the vastness of forest and sky." A small clump of pine needles at the end of a crooked branch in sharp silhouette against a clear gray background.

"Say, look, Mr.—?" Wager held out his hand.

"Flint. Charles Flint." He gave Wager's fingertips a cool squeeze.

"Gabe Villanueva. I'm really interested in photography, man, but I don't know nothing about it. I used to live in West Texas, and the only pictures we had were on the post-office walls. What you're showing me blows my mind, and I'd like to dig it. Maybe we can get a beer and rap a little bit about this?"

The beard folded slightly around Flint's cheeks. "Perhaps some other time, Mr. Villanueva."

"Gabe."

"Gabe. But I spend most of my time here at the gallery. I'll be happy to talk with you sometime when things aren't so rushed. But now is the tourist season, you see."

Wager was genuinely disappointed; he'd have felt more in control sitting in a bar with the comfortable smell of stale beer and frying grease. "Sure, man, I don't mean to push. It's just that you're flashing me things I've never seen. Why don't I buy this one with the tree and take it home and look at it? Maybe I can start seeing what you see in it. Then when things ain't so busy, we can shoot the shit about art and stuff."

The red eyebrows rose. "That's an excellent idea, Gabe!"

"Well, the picture does kind of turn me on. How much?"

Flint looked at the back of the small cardboard square. "Thirty-five."

He managed to keep smiling. "Fine." Sergeant Johnston would like a nice arty photograph for his wall. Wager peeled two twenties off the thick roll and felt Flint's eyes follow it as he stuffed the money back into his jeans. "And I'll drop by for that rap soon."

But it couldn't be too soon; instead, it was back to the bar stools to sip flat suds and wait until, after a while, the big, low-roofed room of the Timber Line Tavern began to feel as familiar as the Frontier down in Denver, bringing that relaxation that comes from rubbing past the same corners again and again. The paneling, the bar stanchions and beams of peeled logs, the fieldstone fireplace in use even on August evenings spoke the idea of mountain cabins and vast pine forests. And that made the waiting almost tolerable.

Chandler had been right about Nederland being closed to outsiders, even during the tourist season. In addition to Flint, Wager had seen half a dozen faces he recognized from mug shots and Chandler's descriptions; but he couldn't just step right up and say, "Let's deal." In Denver, in Boulder, in a dozen other towns in the state, all he had to do was stop to tie his shoe on a certain corner or in certain parks and some dude would murmur, "Pot? Speed? Hash? How about a little acid?" Up in Aspen, he'd even seen coke dealers splitting a baggie in the middle of the street! Here, Wager had not even been offered a joint. It was as if, after the close one Farnsworth had with Rietman and Chandler, the town's dealers were paranoid.

He gave it another week of sporadic sitting and gabbing with one bartender after another, until, finally, his patience blistering from hard rubbing, he went back to Denver and began to telephone from his apartment.

"Suzy? Can you get Hansen for me?"

"He's on pager—are you at home?"

"Yes."

Hansen called back in ten minutes. "Hey, stranger! How's things on the Western Slope?"

"Fine, Rog. I need a favor."

"You've got it."

"Do any of your C.I.s have contacts up in Nederland?"

"Nederland? I thought you were in Aspen?"

"You know how one thing leads to another."

"Right. Well, I can find out. You don't want to use your own stable?"

"No. And I don't want my name on it, either. If you've got somebody, let me know and I'll take it from there."

51

The call came the next morning as Wager was frying hash and eggs. "I got two who say they know how to buy from people in Nederland."

"Just a minute, the hash is burning. . . . O.K., what's happening?"

"These two say they know a couple people that operate out of Nederland. They're not regular suppliers and they're not that big, but they show up with stuff every now and then."

"Did they give you names?"

"You ready for this? Bruce the Juice Hornbacher, and Big Mac."

"Jesus. All we need now is a bottle of ketchup. Can I meet one of your people?"

A pause. "I guess so."

The hesitation was understandable—a detective's C.I.s were his private property. "A phone call from either one would be O.K."

"Why don't I just have one of them set it up? All he has to do is tell Bruce the Juice you're interested. Hell, you don't even have to see my people for that."

That would be even better. "Tell them to make a meet as soon as they can."

"What do you want to buy?"

"Oh, something easy. LSD—five hundred hits. Tell them I'll go as high as two hundred for it."

"That's better than market price."

"Yeah, it's government scale. Tell him to make it as soon as he can."

Another day passed; Wager moved restlessly from his small balcony to the faintly echoing living room and back to the balcony. Near noon, he telephoned Sergeant Johnston because there was no one else to telephone.

"What have you got, Gabe?"

"Nothing. The place's tight as a cherry."

"Pot? Speed?"

"Not a thing. I'm trying to get one of Hansen's C.I.s to put me in touch with somebody up there."

"Do you think the C.I. will keep his mouth shut?"

"He'd better. Besides, he won't know much."

"Just don't get sacked."

"Right, Ed."

"Oh, Suzy's got a message—hang on."

A moment later she picked up another extension. "Gabe? There's somebody in Colorado Springs who's been calling every day."

He read her the number by his telephone. "Is that the one?"

"Yes."

"I'll get on it." He dialed long distance and charged the call to the O.C.D. office number. The cautious mumble answered, "Hello?"

"This is Gabe."

"Say—you left me sitting on my ass for a long time!"

"I've been out of town, Ernie."

"Yeah, well you know I don't work with nobody else but you, man, and there's this big operation that's been going on I heard about."

Some snitches felt safer working with an agent from out of town; Ernie was one of them. "What operation?"

"I heard about some people who got a big lab set up—a whole fucking factory for turning out MDA."

This was a liquid hallucinogenic dropped, like LSD, on blotter tabs or sugar cubes or even dough balls or chewing gum. But such a big operation was puzzling, "I haven't heard about much of that crap around here."

"They don't sell locally—that's their cover. They ship it out to the Coast. Like to L.A., San Diego, San Jose. They got good cover: it's Petroleum Chemical Supply. That way they can order the chemicals to make the stuff, and nobody knows. They're even in the phone book—look it up, man."

Sometimes it happened this way, but not very damned of-

53

ten; he took notes as he talked. "How did you get the word?"

"I got a friend came in from L.A. He's a real vision freak: mushrooms, peyote, chemicals, the whole bag. He knows about these dudes from out there. He says they have quality merchandise."

"Is this friend reliable?"

"You know me, Gabe. I wouldn't call you on bullshit."

Not always, that was true. "Have you seen any of it?"

"No way, man, and I don't want to. I got to watch my local reputation. You hear about that guy they found shot down here? The word's out he was, you know, an informant."

"I heard." If Ernie didn't have direct knowledge of the factory, that made the tip hearsay—he'd need something more solid for a valid search warrant. No matter who they caught or what they found, if they didn't have a good search warrant, any lawyer could suppress the evidence at the advisement stage. And no evidence meant no case. "Is your friend still in town?"

"He was when you called the first time. That's why I couldn't talk. But he's split now, back to L.A. I couldn't get aholt of you, man!"

"Do you have his address?"

"Listen, don't tie me in on this! You ain't forgot our deal?"

"No, I ain't forgot. But I need direct evidence for a search warrant. No warrant, no juice; no juice for us, no bread for you."

He could hear quiet breathing. Finally Ernie whispered, "All right. But, man, you got to get to him without saying who tipped you; I mean, he's my *friend*, you know?"

"He won't hear your name. He maybe won't have to come back here. All we need for a probable cause warrant is a deposition from a witness, and we can handle that through the officers out there."

"Yeah, well, you better hustle, though. These dudes don't stay set up for long in one place."

When he telephoned his information to Johnston, the ser-

54

geant had the same reaction as Gabe. "It sounds too good to be true."

*"Eso vale su precio."*

"What?"

"It's cheap at the price."

"I guess it is. But what about manpower? Hansen and Ashcroft are already putting in twenty, thirty hours overtime, and we sure as hell don't want to fumble the ball up in Nederland. Even for this. Maybe we should let the Springs handle it."

They could just turn it over to D.E.A. or to the Pikes Peak regional drug unit. But Ernie trusted Wager; he had been a good C.I. in the past, and to turn the case over to another unit would toss Ernie away. "You really want that?"

"No. It's your tip and you got the right to be in on it."

And that gave O.C.D. a right to the credit, too. "I've been sitting on my tail for two weeks wasting the taxpayer's money. If this is as cut-and-dried as it sounds, it shouldn't take long."

"Let me ask the inspector. I'll get back to you."

It took less than five minutes. "The inspector's hot to go, Gabe; it seems somebody up in D.E.A. told the Denver office to cool it about the Rietman thing and to work—what was the word?—amicably? Anyway, to cooperate fully with the local agencies."

"We kiss and make up?"

"That's it. The inspector's asking D.E.A. to get a foursquare deposition from L.A. He wants to see how sincere they are. As soon as it's here, they'll pick up a warrant and send an agent over."

"Good. I'll call back." Wager began to feel like a cop again, and it was good.

Hansen called just before supper. "One of my C.I.s tried to set you up with Bruce the Juice, but the son of a bitch is cagey. He won't meet you unless my man comes along."

"So?"

"Well, my C.I. says no."

"Your C.I. said 'no'!"

"Yeah, Gabe. I'm sorry."

Sorry, shit. That C.I. might be in Hansen's stable, but by God Wager needed him. "Can I talk to your man?"

"You really want him that bad?"

He wouldn't ask if it wasn't so. "I do."

"He'll probably want me to come along."

"Where can we meet? Tonight."

"I'll call back."

Hansen wasn't happy, and that was too God damned bad. But he called anyway, just as Wager was rinsing the few supper dishes and stacking them in the dishwasher with the breakfast stuff. "Suppose we see you over at Forty-second and York at ten."

It was as good a place as any—a mixture of residential and commercial, where cars parked along dark streets wouldn't draw attention. "Fine."

Wager's sedan was there before the hour, the radio pack under the front seat quietly monitoring the action of Denver's District 1. A few minutes after ten, Hansen came up on the primary channel: "Two-one-two, what's your ten-twenty?"

"East of York on Forty-second," said Wager.

"Ten-seventy-seven in five minutes."

"O.K."

He slumped in the seat to lower his profile against the dim glow of a streetlight and the glaring lights of busy York street; within the five minutes, he saw Hansen's pale blue Plymouth swing off York and cruise past, the circle of a face turned toward his car. Wager clicked his transmit button twice and the blue car wheeled around in front of a low brick building marked "GORDON'S BOOKS, WHOLESALE ONLY." It pulled up behind him, and the lights were turned off. Wager got out and walked to Hansen's car.

The detective's face lifted from the dark window. "Hi,

Gabe. This is Larry." Wager nodded at the shadowy figure across the seat. "He said he'd hear what you had to say."

"That's real nice." Wager smelled cheap, sweet bourbon on Larry's breath. The profile showed a round skull with straight hair slicked back to curl in a little feathery ledge at the thin nape. He was new to Wager.

"Roger here tells me you want to lay one on the Juice."

"No. On his suppliers."

"I don't know, man. I never had much to do with the Juice."

"Just tell him your regular contact ran out and you've got a heavy customer to supply."

"I don't know. It might look funny."

"It'll look a hell of a lot funnier if I go pop this Juice and say you were the one who put me on him."

"Hey, what's this shit? Hansen, you told me this guy just wanted to talk about things!"

"Cool it, Gabe. We can work something out."

Who the hell was in whose stable? "I need that contact, Rog. It is God damned important."

"I know, I know. Look, Larry, you'll be covered by Bruce the Juice, right? Gabe doesn't even want the guy—he's not big enough. He just wants to use him for an in."

"Yeah, well, Bruce'll remember who brought him in, too. I mean the Juice ain't dumb, you know." The voice dropped slightly: "Besides, I don't dig getting hassled, you know what I mean? I don't have to put up with that shit—I don't owe him shit, or anybody else."

Wager leaned forward to get a good view of the thin face.

"What are you looking at?"

Wager smiled widely. "You. People always need favors sooner or later, and I want to remember you good when you need a favor. I want to remember you said you didn't owe anybody anything."

"Hey, now . . . Hey, now . . ."

"Come on, Gabe, just let me talk to him!"

"Larry, you maybe don't owe me nothing, but I can fix it so you'll look over your shoulder every time you goddam jaywalk. I can fix it so you can't goddam take a piss without breaking some law."

"Hey, now!"

"Come on, Gabe!"

"I'll wait in my car for two minutes, Larry. Either the deal goes down or you do."

It took less than a minute. Hansen, a shadow in the streetlight, bent to Wager's window. "He's a good C.I., Gabe, and he's mine."

"One cop's C.I. is another cop's crook—you know that. And they'd better."

"But he's still a human being, Gabe, and goddamn it, you didn't need to lean on him to make him do it. He just likes to mouth off a little. I could have talked him into it."

"He's scum. If you don't step on scum, it steps on you. When is he taking me up to Nederland?"

"Jesus, Gabe." Hansen's shadow slowly shook its head. "He'll call Bruce. It'll be sometime this weekend."

"Good."

Both calls came two days later: Hansen telephoning for his snitch ("Larry's still a little pissed off—he, ah, wanted me to let you know the meet's set"), and Sergeant Johnston saying the deposition had arrived and the warrant was being made out. "Kickoff's in three hours."

It was 2 P.M. now. "I'm supposed to be in Boulder at nine."

Johnston thought it over. "You don't have to be in on this —it's up to you."

"I'd like to—I'm tired of just farting around. Suppose me and the D.E.A. people go down and look over the place now and you bring the warrant when it's ready?"

"No, we have to get a lab tech, too. We'd better all go together." Johnston also sounded tired of just sitting. "I'll try to hurry things up. Come on over to the office and we'll leave as soon as possible."

A little more than two hours later, as Wager and Johnston walked past the inspector's door on the way to their car, Sonnenberg called out, "Are you going to the Springs now?"

"Yes, sir," Johnston answered. "D.E.A. said the warrant's on its way down, and Gabe has to be in Boulder tonight. We're going over to the lab and pick up Mrs. Nelson now."

Sonnenberg reached for his coat. "Give me your keys—I'll drive. I'm damned tired of just sitting around this office."

"You, sir?"

"Is something wrong with that?"

"No, sir, but . . ." Sergeant Johnston shut up.

They stopped at the police laboratory and the sergeant went in for Mrs. Nelson. A squarely built woman in a dark pants suit, she smiled shyly at Wager and Sonnenberg as Johnston introduced them. "Is there room for my kit back here?"

"Yes, ma'am," said Wager, grunting to lift the red toolbox across the seat.

"All set?" asked Sonnenberg, and had the car rolling before Johnston had shut his door. The car filled with cigar smoke as the inspector leaned it through the Sixth Avenue interchange onto I-25 South. "It's a beautiful day for a bust! We should have brought Suzy. Has she ever participated in field operations?"

"No, sir, but—"

"Well, next time something like this happens, let's get her out. It's good for morale."

"Yes, sir," said Johnston. "I'll try to set something up."

The inspector made it sound like a picnic instead of business; Wager didn't think he should take it so casually. He had noticed it before: when a tip came too easily, everybody seemed to think it was a goddam picnic.

"How are you doing with Farnsworth, Gabe?"

He told him.

"It's really that closed up there?"

"Yes, sir."

The inspector frowned and drove in silence. "Keep at it for a while, anyway. God knows we could use you here, but Farnsworth would be a big feather in our cap."

As if Wager didn't know. "Yes, sir."

They began to clear the underpasses of downtown. Over the lowering banks of the freeway, clusters of raw and treeless apartments, condominiums, sprawling split-level houses gradually thinned into gray-green clumps of sagebrush and the yellowing buffalo grass of late summer.

"Where did D.E.A. say they would meet us?"

"At Fillmore Street, sir."

"Did they say who they were sending?"

"No, sir."

"Well, I hope they're there. I don't want to wait all day for them."

"Yes, sir."

The inspector radioed the Highway Patrol to clear his passage, then set the speedometer needle on ninety. "Great day for a bust!"

From the back seat, Wager saw the muscles in Sergeant Johnston's neck tense; and despite the smile in his own mind at the sergeant's fear, he had to force himself to look relaxed for Mrs. Nelson. She was wide-eyed enough without seeing anxiety in him. If he had been driving, he would have been relaxed; but, like a lot of trained drivers, he never trusted anyone else behind the wheel, and that unease was compounded by an embarrassment that came with hearing the inspector chatter like an excited rookie. An inspector's place was at his desk where he gave orders, asked hard questions, and kept the politicians off your back. Excitement just wasn't professional.

The D.E.A. had not yet made it to the rendezvous; and during the half-hour they had to wait, the inspector asked twice, "Where are they?" and Sergeant Johnston answered twice, "I don't know, sir." It was a stupid question and a stupid answer, and everybody, including Mrs. Nelson, knew it. Wager began to wish he hadn't come along. At last, a car whose absence of color or ornament marked it as official twisted down the off-ramp and pulled into the parking area behind a gas station where they sat. One of two men stepped out of the car. Wager didn't recognize either agent, though Sonnenberg did: "That's Petersen, assistant to the regional director. It looks as if they wanted to have seniority over us. It'll make him over-joyed to see me." Sonnenberg got out and shook hands. Wager, Johnston, and the lab tech waited while the men smiled at each other and then Sonnenberg introduced them to Petersen. Finally all the preliminaries were over.

"We've got the warrant, Inspector Sonnenberg. Do you want to follow us over?"

"Sergeant Johnston knows the town. Why don't we lead, Agent Petersen?"

Only the slightest hesitation. "Fine, Inspector." D.E.A. was cooperating amicably with local agencies.

Johnston, a map of Colorado Springs spread on his knees, guided the inspector east to Academy Boulevard and then south toward the municipal airport. They entered one of those light-industrial areas made up of sprawling one-story buildings and fenced storage yards. This late in the afternoon, the streets were drained of cars, and only an occasional tiny home not yet bought for business purposes brought any life to the area. Sonnenberg swung once around an almost windowless cinder-block building squatting on a corner. A chain-link fence marked the bare back yard; a black-and-white sign over the door said, "PETROLEUM CHEMICAL SUPPLY." The inspector keyed his transmitter: "Can you cover the rear of the building? I'll put one of my people on the yard side and one on the street side."

Wager felt better; the silly excitement of the ride down had been replaced by the calm, slow voice that came when the inspector was really concentrating on a case.

"My man will be back there. I'll see you at the front door."

Petersen would be amicable, but he wouldn't surrender. The D.E.A. vehicle turned out of sight. Sonnenberg glanced at Wager. "You cover this side. Ed, you take the yard side. Mrs. Nelson, you just sit tight in the car."

Wager nodded and slid out of the vehicle. This wall of the gray building had only two windows, both closed and high off the ground. He placed himself at the corner nearest the front door in case the inspector and Petersen needed a quick backup; the D.E.A. vehicle returned and the two cars swung quickly into the shallow parking area at the building's front. "Check in" came over his radio, and he waited his turn: "Two-one-two, set."

"Going in."

The slam of the car doors was followed by quick steps in the gravel, making Wager aware of just how quiet the buildings and yards were. He rested his hand on the familiar .45 Star tucked out of sight under the tail of his sport coat and waited.

The inspector's voice popped on the radio. "The front door's locked and barred. Ed, do you or Gabe have access?"

"There's a door over here," said Johnston. "It's got a window I can knock out."

"Let me get around to cover you."

"Ten-four."

The shatter of glass, followed by more long minutes of silence. Finally, Sonnenberg radioed, "It's empty. We'll see you at the front door."

Johnston let them in; a sharp chemical smell stung deep into Wager's sinuses, and his shoes crackled loudly on the almost vacant concrete floor.

"I think we've got something!" The inspector's voice bounced around a fiberboard partition along one wall. "Ed, get the technician in here."

The sergeant brought her in; the embarrassment was gone and she walked quickly, leaning against the heavy pull of the toolbox. "This way, ma'am; I think we really scored."

The working part of the laboratory was set on a long bench blocked from any accidental view through the windows. Spaced along the shelf were five glass beakers the size of basketballs; scattered here and there and stoppered with corks or covered with aluminum foil were smaller jars and beakers, all of which held liquids or powders. Among the scattered work gloves, paper towels, glass tubes, and stirring rods, hoses and clips led from one container to another.

"Sweet Jesus," said Petersen. "I've never seen a lab this big!"

The technician studied the setup and then busily drew a sample from the last beaker filled with thick white powder; the liquid reagent slid into the test tube and she swirled it slightly, lifting the glass against the overhead light. "It colors, Inspector."

"Ex-cel-lent! Is it MDA?"

"It's of that family. I'll have to run laboratory tests to determine the exact composition. But it's enough for presumptive positive."

"I'd like to send some down to our Dallas lab, too," said Petersen.

"We got plenty," said Johnston.

"Do you know what this stuff sells for?" The other D.E.A. man scratched in the clipped hair of his head and stared at the beaker. "On the street, it's three dollars a dose; and you figure maybe ten thousand doses to an ounce of pure powder. And there must be thirty pounds of shit—pardon me, ma'am—stuff in that one jug!"

Wager stared. Even wholesale, this shelf of goodies ran almost $200,000. And this was just one shipment. Of how many? "How long does it take to turn out a jar of the stuff?"

Mrs. Nelson glanced up from the evidence label she was filling in. "The way the process is set up, they can turn out thirty pounds every twelve hours." She pointed her pencil at two other beakers filled with opaque liquid. "That's going through the final stage now. After desication, each flask should produce about ten pounds of powder."

Two hundred thousand dollars every twelve hours! "Wow," said Wager, and he meant it. "That's almost a day's pay for an honest cop. And all tax-free."

"There's a tax," said Sonnenberg. "I aim to tax these people ten or fifteen years. Agent Petersen, can you have your local man get out a John Doe warrant for the owners and/or operators of this establishment?"

"You bet I can." He strode quickly to his car and its radio.

"By gosh, Gabe." The inspector lit a fresh cigar, the odor of its tobacco resting sluggishly on the sharper chemical smell. "You've got your hands on a good C.I.—let's give him top pay."

"Yes, sir," he said, thinking of Bruce the Juice and Larry. "I wish I had more like him."

# 5

The meet with Bruce the Juice took place in Boulder's Chautauqua Park. It was the kind of area where the dark and narrow roads were lined with cars whose occupants—neckers, underage beer drinkers, dope dealers—could see any trouble coming across the grassy moonlit lawns. Larry was still sulking, but at least the whiskey smell was gone.

"I don't know you after this, Officer Gabe whatever-your-name-is."

"Don't get my hopes up."

"I just plain don't like you, you know what I mean?"

"Tough shit."

The conversation faltered.

Through the darkness, the tilting slabs of the giant Flatiron Rocks could scarcely be made out, but their weight loomed just beyond the trees as one might feel a wall in a black room.

Floating on the warm night air that began to lift from the prairie to wash against the Front Range came the tinny voices of the park's summer movie series, the steady rustle of distant traffic from the valley below, the pulsing howl of a faraway siren. From one of the shadowy cars that had slid past and parked ten or fifteen minutes ago, a dim figure emerged and walked slowly toward them.

"That looks like him. Yeah, that's him."

"Just take it easy, Larry. Just play it natural."

"Yeah. With you around."

The shadow leaned to Larry's window. "That you, man?"

"You know it. This here's Gabe."

"Hey, man."

Wager grunted, "Get in—we been waiting."

"Yeah, well, can't be too careful, man."

"You have the stuff?"

"Not on me. But I can have it here in a half-hour. Where's the front money?"

"Larry didn't tell me nothing about fronting—just a straight deal."

"It's my thing with new people, man. I'm very big on security."

Wager hesitated; there was a dealer's saying, "Never front the coin until you got the crap," and anyone in the business would know the truth of that. But he'd waited a long time for this contact. He slowly peeled five twenties from the roll of bills, letting Bruce see the size of the wad of money. "I'll front half."

The shadow's arm reached across the seat back. "Cool."

Wager held a corner of the bills before letting them go. "I know you're not going to rip me off—it ain't worth losing a good customer for just a hundred bucks."

"Right, man—it ain't that much of a deal."

The door closed after him, and his car turned out through the stone pillars of the park gate. Wager and Larry sat in silence. In twenty minutes, the car swung back and pulled in behind them. Bruce the Juice came to Wager's window. "Here you go, man—tablets." He palmed the plastic baggie at Wager, who took his time, snapping a tablet in two and looking carefully at its color under the dash light, touching it with his tongue for any taste. He handed the second roll of twenties to Bruce. "If my customers like it, I'll be back. I'm very big on customer satisfaction."

"Cool."

"You got a telephone?"

"Yeah, 258–4453. Just leave a number and I'll call you back. That's my old lady's phone, and I don't do business on it."

Wager would wait a full week before making the call; it was like fishing with a light line: you couldn't pull too hard or you'd lose it all. On Wednesday, he checked in at the O.C.D. office. Mrs. Gutierrez, at her little window, was worried until he came close enough to be recognized. "My, Detective Wager! You do look different!"

"Yes, ma'am."

And Suzy just giggled and said, "A necklace?"

Wager didn't think there was much to laugh at. "Is Sergeant Johnston in?"

She nodded and turned quickly back to the typewriter. Which remained suspiciously silent.

"Morning, Ed. Here's something I been meaning to bring you." He handed him the photograph of the tree.

He turned it first one way, then another. "What is it?"

"The isolated individual confronting the mystery of darkness. Hang it on your wall." He pointed to the stretch of plywood spotted with framed diplomas, membership scrolls, certificates, and awards. "Give the place a little class."

Johnston looked at it again and then handed it back. "I don't have too much room in here."

"It's state property now. I sure hate to just throw it away."

"State property? What'd it cost you?"

Wager told him.

"Thirty-five bucks!" Johnston looked at it once more. "For that much, we can't afford to throw it away. Hang it out there by the office door. Your office needs more class than mine, anyway."

"Maybe I'd better ask Suzy first."

"Just don't let the inspector know how much it cost."

"What's the latest on the MDA factory?"

"Jesus and Mary, haven't I seen you since then?" His fingers moved across his freckled scalp and then patted down the limp red hairs. "Say, we really scored—it turns out the John Does were a couple guys the D.E.A.'s been after for three years. They had a factory up near Fort Collins and then moved to Pueblo, and then they moved again before D.E.A. could get a lead on them. The inspector's really high about getting to them before the feds."

"That's fine. All that stuff was for real?"

"You better believe it! When the D.A. down in the Springs saw all the crap we had in our evidence locker, he couldn't believe his eyes."

"Since we're going to court on it, I should pay off the snitch."

Johnston reached for a voucher. "How much?"

Wager shrugged. "A thousand?"

"Do you think that's high enough? That was a hell of a big haul."

"I don't want to spoil him. Make it fifteen hundred. He'll be real happy with that."

"O.K."

Wager took the fifteen-hundred-dollar voucher and the thirty-five-dollar photograph to his desk and gazed around at the walls cluttered with various official scrolls. If he hung the picture where Johnston wanted, he'd have it in front of him whenever he sat at his desk. But behind his back, on the wall that hid the stairs going up to the attic storage area, there was a good spot. It would be in front of Hansen then. "You got a thumbtack, Suzy?"

"Here. What's that?"

"A little art. We're going to have us a little class."

"Gee, that's a good one! I didn't know you were into photography."

"What's a good one?"

"The picture—it's like somebody standing all alone, and night's coming on."

Wager studied the print. "You really think so? Why?"

"Well, the white trunk: no leaves, but it's still standing solidly, almost glowing against the darkness, like it knew what was happening to it, but it's daring the softer trees to come after it. Did you take it?"

"No, I bought it. It cost thirty-five dollars!"

"Well it's sure worth it. Maybe I'll bring in some of my shots sometime. Maybe you'd like to see them."

"Sure—that sounds good." He had never wondered what Suzy did when she wasn't working; all of her family was back in Wisconsin or Michigan or somewhere, and she wasn't pretty enough to have boyfriends. Not that she was really bad; just that she was like a stretch of flat road—nothing to notice. It was strange to imagine her as an amateur photographer or as anything else other than Suzy, secretary for the Narc Section. "You really think it's worth thirty-five dollars? I mean it's just a picture."

"Yes. It makes a clear statement, and the technical aspect's good, too. I like the way the light-on-dark gives it depth—it makes the dead tree come toward you, so that you get a feeling of how solid and determined it still is."

"Oh." He handed the cardboard to her. "Maybe you'd better hang it, then. You'll do a better job."

"If you want me to." She busied herself with a couple of loops of Scotch tape, "This way there're no holes in the frame," and then studied the wall. Finally she stepped back. "Is it straight?"

Wager looked up from dialing the telephone; it was the happiest note he had ever heard in her voice, and he felt in some obscure way that he had played a mean trick on her. "It really does look fine, Suzy."

The bell rattled at the other end of the line; after four rings, Ernie's cautious whisper said, "Yeah?"

"This is Gabe."

"Hey, I saw it in the paper—pictures and everything. The inspector said it was the biggest lab he'd ever seen. What's his name? Songbird?"

"Sonnenberg."

"Yeah, him. How come your picture didn't get in? Hey, that was a big bust. Did I lead you right or did I lead you right?"

"It was a good tip, Ernie. I'm mailing you a token of appreciation from a grateful citizenry."

"How much is a token?"

"Fifteen hundred."

"Hey! That's all right!"

"Don't act too rich too soon—those dudes are out on bail and are probably very suspicious about a tip."

"Hey, you're right. Maybe you'd better hold on to it awhile. If I get it, I'll spend it sure."

"Put it in the bank and forget about it."

"How the hell can I forget about fifteen hundred bucks? You better hang on to it."

"All right. I'll send it down in four weeks—they'll have had their preliminary hearing and be worried about a hell of a lot more than a tip. You want any now? A couple hundred?"

"Naw, I'm smooth for a while—you keep it. Four weeks, and things'll be cool again."

"Right." He wrote a note for Suzy to process the voucher and send the cash by registered mail in four weeks. Ernie would still have to poor-mouth; the MDA people would have friends.

But there was no sense making him crap his pants by telling him now.

Hansen, moving with the briskness that said action, swung into the office, "Gabe, babe—Lord, you look like something else! How did Larry work out?"

"He didn't like it, but he did it. *Hombre,* if he was in my stable—"

Hansen interrupted, "He works fine for me. You handle yours your way, I'll handle mine my way."

He turned back to his desk. Hansen was right, but that didn't make Wager like it. As he started through the stack of correspondence that Suzy had been saving for him, he heard Hansen dial out, and say, "Willy, Willy, fat and silly—this is your old buddy Rog. What've you got for me?"

At the end of the week, Wager made his call. A child dropped the receiver in his eagerness to answer the telephone, and a moment later an irritated man's voice said, "Hello?"

"Bruce? This is Gabe. We met in that park in Boulder."

"Got a number, man?"

"Yeah, 934–9491. In a half-hour."

"Right, man."

It was the pay-phone number in his apartment lobby, seldom used at all and never in the afternoon. Bruce the Juice would probably call from a pay phone also. Wiretaps, like other ways of gathering evidence, went through cycles: for a while they would work fine; then dealers would be paranoid about wiretaps; then they would forget the wiretaps as some other means began to surface in court. This seemed to be a paranoid phase. Smart dealers, usually those higher up than Bruce, set up meets from different public telephones—and as far as Gabe knew, no judge had yet granted a warrant to tap a public phone. He lifted the receiver on the first ring. "Hello?"

"Who's this?"

"Gabe."

"Sorry for asking, man, but I don't know your voice yet."

Wager heard the background noise of tires on gravel and the clink of a gas-station bell. "Just do your thing, Juice. We're all in this together." More than you know.

"Right on. I'll see you at Sugarloaf Road and Boulder Canyon in two hours. You know where it's at?"

"I'll find it."

Gabe drove his pickup west and then swung north along the Foothills Highway to Boulder. It was one of those mid-September afternoons when autumn was noticed for the first time. The light was hazy and soft with thin dust, and over the highway and wheeling through the long afternoon shadows of the mountains, white specks of sea gulls glided across empty yellow prairies. When the sea gulls came to feed on the grasshoppers, summer was at an end. He remembered that from his boyhood, when it had been a short walk from home to open fields and ranchland, and even now some of the old feeling came back: the excitement of school about to begin, the restlessness and unease that was maybe part of all animals after the sun had begun to swing south, the sense of loss for a summer that was never long enough. Now the tourists were gone and the roads empty in a midafternoon light that held more glow than heat; the Front Range seemed to jut up sharper in this quiet time, and Wager felt more keenly the obscenity of the people who made his work necessary. All this beauty, this sunlight and air, this solid quietness, and it wasn't enough for them. They wanted things that only a lot of money could buy —fast money from stupid children, from high-school kids spoiled for kicks and good times, from college kids and young swingers who already had more than they could value, from old men and women whose kicks and good times had gone, leaving them with a hunger to be numb to what was left them, from skinny addicts drifting big-eyed and filthy like flies through the garbage of Denver. And they saw it all as a game—a game of profit and loss, overhead and net and gross; a game of cops-and-robbers. Maybe that was what he disliked most: that he had to play a game, too.

The junction, a single road to the right, was a short way up Boulder Canyon; Wager pulled in behind a sagging 1969 Buick, faded green roof over a cream body scraped and patched with rust. License ML 3109. Bruce the Juice got out and came to the truck window. In the sunlight, he looked even younger than he had seemed in the dark of Chautauqua Park: medium height, thin build, brown eyes, struggling yellow beard, and hair bleached into strips of light and dark and tied in a long ponytail down his back.

"Just leave your truck here, man. We'll go in my car."

Wager rolled up the windows and locked the doors. Bruce watched him.

"What's the matter, man? No trust in humanity?"

"I got this thing about security," Wager said, smiling.

They drove silently for half a mile or so, Bruce swinging the spongy sedan through the sharp bends up Sugarloaf Hill. At a graveled turnout on a spur high over the valley, he slowed to a stop. "So let's deal."

"What do you handle?"

"I run a full-service drugstore; you name it, I either got it or I can get it."

"How about an ounce of clean snort?"

The Juice was silent a moment and Wager wondered if he'd come on too fast. "You got the customers for that?"

He could almost hear the thought behind the question: anybody dealing in that much cocaine should have a reputation, and the Juice never heard of Gabe. "That's what I'm in business for. The people I talk with say they want to try coke. What's your price?"

"Twenty-five hundred."

"Screw that—I got to make a living, too. I can't build up

customers if my overhead's too high."

"This is close to eighty percent, man. And even whores don't give it away."

Wager shook his head and hoped he was playing it right. "Maybe I'm just a poor dumb Texas boy, but no way am I gonna get ripped off like that. Give me a fair price or I'll look up somebody else."

"Cool it, babe, cool it! I had to find out if you're legitimate. A narc would've paid that without blinking. How's two thousand sound?"

"That makes a sound like going down. You got it on you?"

"No way. I only carry the merchandise on a confirmed deal. And a deal ain't confirmed until I count the money." He looked at Wager. "Well?"

He dug into the back pocket of his Levis for the wad of bills. "You can see it, you can touch it, you can count it. But you don't get nothing until I test the dope. It's a lot of money this time." Wager smoothed out the flash roll on his thigh and leafed through the bills slowly. "Satisfied?"

"Right on." He started the car and swung out to the narrow blacktop heading back into Boulder Canyon. "I'll see you in an hour at the North Broadway shopping center. I'll park in the southwest corner of the lot."

"I'll be there."

"Anything else your customers want? Speed, acid, grass, hash?"

"Grass is no problem—they can get that anywhere."

"I carry quality merchandise. There may be some as good, but there ain't none better, man. I can even get Hawaiian pot, and if your customers ain't tried that, they ain't really had good stuff."

"All right. Give me a lid and I'll see how they like it. Mescaline or peyote—you got any of that?"

"In a couple days. It sounds like you're servicing a bunch of dippers. Most people can't hack that stuff more'n once."

Wager smiled. "They're willing to pay, I'm willing to deal."

"That's business, ain't it?" He stopped beside Wager's truck. "Anything you need, I can get. We'll catch your act in an hour."

"Right."

He arrived at the crowded parking lot a bit early and waited, his rear-view mirror capturing occasional housewives rattling shopping carts from the supermarket, towing stiff-armed children through the hesitant cars nosing for parking spaces. The old Buick finally entered the lot from Broadway, circled once through the sun-glinting traffic, and then disappeared behind a panel truck two rows away from Wager. He walked to it and sat in the rider's seat. Bruce the Juice handed him a brown lunch bag. Inside lay a wrapper of cocaine and a plastic baggie of loose marijuana. Wager unwrapped a homemade reagent kit, using a glass rod to dip a film of the powder into the tiny bottle.

"You make that kit yourself?"

"Yeah." He shook the mixture and then studied its color.

"There's an outfit in L.A. that manufactures real ones. You ought to get yourself one. There's a head shop in Denver that sells them. You can test all sorts of dope with it, man."

"I'm glad to hear that," said Wager.

"How's it look?"

"It looks fine." He handed Bruce the thick roll of twenties and waited while he counted them. "How much for the grass?"

"It's yours, man. If your customers like it, buy from me. If not"—Bruce's thin blond beard parted in a smile—"I'll take it off my advertising account."

On his way home, Wager stopped by the custodian's office to drop off the dope. The civilian employee—Elizabeth M. Miller, as her name tag reminded him—looked as if she had not slept very well. She handed him an evidence envelope. Wager was finishing the date and time line when a familiar voice spoke over his shoulder: "Liz, honey, got time for a cup?"

"Hello, Rog," said Wager.

Hansen started. "Gabe? Good Lord, I can't get used to the way you look. Say, you got some goodies! Do you know Liz? Liz Miller—Gabe Wager. He's one of the best agents in the O.C.D."

Wager nodded to the girl, whose smile was a little too tight and forced; it seemed to fit her need for sleep. "Pleased to meet you," he said shortly; he did not like high-strung broads.

"Got time for some coffee? Liz and me are going for a cup."

Wager shook his head and pushed the evidence envelope across the counter to the young woman, who logged it in. He turned to Hansen, "I would like to talk to you for a minute."

They stepped a few feet down the hall, and leaned against the tan walls out of the way of the corridor traffic. "I want you to drop the word that there's a Mr. Taco doing business."

"Who's that?"

"Me."

"Ha. That's a good one—I didn't know you made jokes. What kind of word do you want out?"

"Ask a few people if they know anything about Mr. Taco. Say, 'I hear he's dealing, I want to know something about him.' That's all. Ask Fat Willy, ask your snitches; have them ask around, too." The name, the question, the assumption would spread like oil through the drug community; in a week or two, Mr. Taco would be a fact; in a month, some snitch would swear he could set him up for a buy and bust.

"Any specialty?"

"No. And don't be too specific. Just the name's enough."

"It sure is. Say, are you onto something?"

"Just a foot in the door. There's still a long way to go."

Wager let another week pass before he set up a third buy from Bruce, this time heroin and mescaline. And another week for a fourth. And another for a fifth. Between buys, he went through the motions with the paperwork that never stopped and that Suzy seemed to think was important enough to place in the center of his desk. Wager wondered if, when he died, he'd crawl into his coffin, and there—in the middle of the satin cushion—would be a pile of papers with Suzy's note, "Gabe, please rush."

Sergeant Johnston looked more and more worried each time Wager submitted a receipt for the week's buy. "This is over nine thousand dollars, Gabe. I hope to God we reach the end zone soon."

"First and ten, do it again."

"What?"

"It's only the first quarter of play, Ed. Don't get tight now, or you might fumble the game away."

"What game?"

"The Farnsworth game, Ed."

"Oh. Ha-ha."

"I want another civilian vehicle, too. Make it a Duster or something like that. Metallic green's a nice color."

"What the hell do you want with another car? That truck's only two months old!"

"I'm a successful dealer—I'm rich." He looked at the figures in his small notebook. "In these five weeks, I would've made twenty-two thousand dollars' profit. I can afford a new car."

"Maybe you can, but I don't know if the department can." He picked up the telephone. "The Inspector had better decide this one."

The answer was yes. "White upholstery," Wager said as he left. "It goes real good with metallic green. Mr. Taco is moving up in the world; he's now *un chulo grande.*"

"Mr. Taco?" Sergeant Johnston's pencil paused over the vehicle request form. *"Chulo?"*

"It's all part of the game, Ed."

"Yeah? Well, you ain't getting a new car unless we can find one in the police lot. The inspector says. And you're by God going to earn it, too—I'm putting you on routine surveillance when you're not chasing Farnsworth. We're so goddam short-

77

handed that we're paying more in overtime, than in straight wages."

Another week went by, this one faster; and Wager was glad to pass the time as part of routine surveillance teams scattered on different cases across the city. Some officers would bitch about it, but Gabe felt more at home slumped in a car seat and listening to the police frequencies than he did prowling around his apartment. At least the taxpayer was getting something for his money, and it made the time pass quicker.

He made two or three runs up to Nederland to dawdle over a beer in the Timber Line. Occasional figures associated with Farnsworth drifted in and out, and once Flint nodded briefly at him. Finally, Bruce the Juice came in followed by a boy about the same age who was even thinner.

"Hey, man, what's happening? What are you doing up this way?"

Wager wagged a hand and pushed a chair with his foot. "I like this place; I didn't know it was your turf."

"Home is where the heart is. Jo-Jo, this is Gabe, the dude I told you about. He's been doing a lot of heavy business with me."

Wager raised his eyebrows.

"No problem, Gabe. Jo-Jo's one of us, man. He's a brother."

Wager grinned lazily. "Let's us brothers have a drink. This here country boy ain't been so fat and happy since it rained in West Texas."

"Cool," said Jo-Jo, and lifted a hand for the bartender. In profile, his narrow face reminded Gabe of a hatchet, forehead and chin slanted back from the pointed tip of his nose. "If Juice ever drops you, let me know. I got a pipeline, too."

Wager looked from one to the other. "I hope you brothers get along O.K."

"Aw, yeah, man," Bruce said, laughing. "No hassles—we don't need to fight over customers. If I ever can't cover you,

Jo-Jo will. This is a good town. Up here, we got no heavies and no shit, you know?"

"And no cops?"

Bruce laughed again. "One marshal, who don't know his ass from his elbow. The sweat comes from the outside—D.E.A. and shit like that."

"Yeah," said Jo-Jo. "Like that son of a bitch Chandler."

"Hey, I warned everybody about that dude, didn't I?" Bruce was annoyed now. "Didn't I say he smelled like a fucking narc the first time I ever saw him?"

Jo-Jo drained his drink and signaled for another round. "You did—and I kiss your ass for that. You sure did. Too goddam bad Farnsworth didn't believe you."

"Farns was lucky."

"What happened?" asked Wager.

"Well," Jo-Jo said, "I guess old Farns thought he was going to rip off this dude Chandler. We all thought he was with the Mafia or something, and—"

"I didn't! I said he was a narc."

"Yeah, anyway, it turned out funny as shit: the dude ran a buy and bust on Farnsworth, and Farns ran a scam on him. The fuzz had to let him go because they bought lactose instead of dope. But it sure as hell blew Chandler out of here. And Goldberg, too—he left the state; he said he had diarrhea for a week after the bust."

"Good riddance," Bruce said. "He was full of crap anyway."

"Does this Farnsworth usually rip people off like that?" Wager asked.

"He never has us," said Bruce. "I never heard of anything like it before. But maybe he smelled something about this deal. Hell, I told him and everybody else right off that Chandler was a narc."

Jo-Jo pushed his sweating glass in a wet circle on the plank table. "I'll tell you this: if Farnsworth ever does get busted, it will leave one hell of a hole around here. Somebody's going to have to fill it."

"Whoa, man," Bruce said. "Let's keep it civilized. We're all doing all right."

"I only said 'if,' Juice." Jo-Jo raised his hand for another round, and Wager traded his half-empty glass of beer for a full cold one.

It had to come sooner or later, and after half a dozen drinks, Jo-Jo, by now twisting his tongue with difficulty around his words, leaned across the table. "Hey, Gabe, old *amigo*, I got some fine stuff in the truck outside. You want to shoot up?"

"No," said Wager. "No, I don't. I burned out four years ago, and I don't want to go back. I'm clean and I want to stay clean."

"So now you deal?"

"That's where the money is. It sure as hell ain't in using."

"Come on, man, just a little pop. It's really smooth stuff."

Wager shook his head.

"Come on, Gabe—we'll hold your hand. Get a new set of wings; it's free, babe!"

"Don't lean on me, Jo-Jo. I can't handle it. Look." He folded his cuff back and showed them the scar of a childhood boil, now a shiny dime of hard flesh inside his forearm. "I had a crater there—and all I did for two years was pour junk in it. Once is enough, so just don't lean all over me, O.K.?"

"Hey, cool it, brother. Jo-Jo was only being polite. We just chip a little in a social way, you know? Nothing heavy—grass, coke, the stuff that won't get you, and maybe a pop now and then. Hell, none of it's as bad as goddam booze. But if it ain't your bag, that's cool—no hassles up here."

Jo-Jo leaned back in his chair, thin lips pressed together in a tight crack. "We don't like hassles. But we ain't afraid of them."

"Cool it, Jo-Jo."

Wager buried his mouth in the glass of beer. The two

younger men watched him. He set the glass squarely back on its ring of water. "What's the matter?"

"Well"—Jo-Jo sniffed and scrubbed under his nose with a grimy knuckle—"me and the Juice here, we been wondering who your customers are. You've handled a lot of stuff, Juice tells me. But I get around and I ain't heard your name on the street anywhere."

Wager held his flesh still against the prickly sensation that began to climb up the back of his neck. It wasn't fear; it was anger. This pimply-faced son of a bitch was trying to come on like Billy Jack. "I've got my route and it's growing." He smiled, and added very quietly, "You looking to take away some of my action, brother?"

"Whoooeee! Juice, this dude's hyped! Look, Pancho, this ain't the first time you been up here. It's a small town, you know? A stranger starts hanging around, the word gets out. Maybe you ain't a narc. If you ain't, the question is why the hell've you been hanging around up here?"

Leaning back in his chair, Wager tried to relax. If anything was coming, it wouldn't be here in the bar. It would be later in a dark corner of the empty lot where his truck was sitting, or halfway down the canyon where the steep rock walls pushed the highway to the edge of the tumbling creek, or at a distant cabin where he'd be invited for a "party." It could happen. But more likely they would just drop him as if he wore a sign around his neck: "DON'T TOUCH—NARC." He would like it better if they tried something. A lot better. It would be a solid pleasure if Jo-Jo tried something. But even that was out: he remembered Rietman's warning, "They got a thing against heavies." So Wager stretched and looked relaxed and tried to bury his angry accent in a smile. "Because I don't like street dealing. Life's too short, man. Did you ever hear of Mr. Taco?"

"Yeah," said Jo-Jo. "Maybe I heard the name around."

"That's me. I've been working only a couple months and already that name's all over the street. How long do you think it would take for the fuzz to ring my bell if I used my own name?"

"No shit," said Bruce. "You're Mr. Taco, the big enchilada?"

Wager grinned wider. "The smiling *sopapilla*—that's me." He brought the chair legs down and leaned across the table, staring hard into Bruce the Juice's eyes, knowing that if he didn't get past this point, there was no way to go but home. "I've finally got some coin, and I've made a few contacts. Now I want to get off the street to where the real money is."

# 6

"Yeah, Gabe, *dinero's* what it's all about." Richard Allen Farnsworth, twenty-eight, dark brown hair pulled tightly back into a stubby pigtail, face made up of two shiny brown eyes, a curving nose whose nostrils lifted slightly at the sides, and a spray of kinky black beard that ran from just under his eyes all the way down his neck. Right now, teeth showed in a smile that clutched the curved stem of a large pipe. A drowsy child, Peter, nodded gently on his rocking knee. "If it was just me and Ramona and Pedrocito, here, I'd quit tomorrow." The pipe bobbed with a short laugh. "In fact, I almost quit when that son of a bitch Chandler did a number on me." Farnsworth wagged his head, a sprig or two of curly hair tugging loose to wag with him.

"What happened?" Wager, heavy from eating too much and spongy from drinking more beer and wine than he was used to, eased first one way and then another on the creaking chair, trying to lift the weight of his own flesh from the wad of food in his stomach. The food, the wine, the sharp-sweet odor of marijuana lingering from Ramona's after-dinner lid made the room bob and wag like Farnsworth's hair and pipe and child; he wanted to reach out and quiet all the motion, to have a moment or two of stasis that would let him fully realize where he really was. But for this long moment, it all seemed like a dream, and Wager felt a jab of fear that he might simply get up and laugh and clap a hand to Farnsworth's bony shoulder and say, "I'm a narc, too," and then stand there grinning at Farnsworth's wide eyes, grinning and waiting to wake up from the dream, the grin slowly draining in icy sweat as he would realize that it wasn't a dream, that he really was in Farnsworth's cabin far from the gritty streets of Denver, that he had really blown his cover.

He was too old for this, too old to take these games seriously; too old not to despise the phony world that made his face the friend of those his mind and heart called enemy; too old to let himself relax and enjoy a good meal and a laugh that was being paid for right now on street corners and in alleys and bars that Farnsworth or Ramona or little Peter would never even see. For now the phony was the real, but when that other world of his mind and heart pressed on him, he felt how slippery was the rock on which he pretended to stand.

"I was set up. Chandler came on like a big buyer from Detroit; sat right there in that chair you're sitting in and smoked a few joints, drank booze, shot the shit with us just like a human being. He had a good rap, man. Smooth and a lot of laughs. Then he wanted a bigger buy than anyone else could handle." The sprigs of wiry hair wagged again. "We thought he was a hit man with the Mafia—Charlie Flint found a gun in the glove compartment of his car and we thought he was a fucking hit man. It never crossed my mind that dude was wearing black boots."

84

"Black boots?"

"Yeah—the sheriff's officers all wear black boots. Uniform regulations. Even the undercover people wear them, because the S.O. doesn't pay those poor bastards enough for two pairs of shoes." He laughed and bobbed the child and sipped at the beer on the small table by his chair. It was Cerveza Tecate; Farnsworth drank only Mexican beer, as a protest against Yankee imperialism. "Those poor bastards got to want something more than money. They're probably all *maricóns* at heart; the boots, the guns, the uniforms—that's the only *cojones* they've got."

"Was Chandler a faggot?"

The pipe snorted a cloud of blue smoke that spread in a flat layer around the living room and slowly drifted toward the Franklin stove sitting out from one corner. From the kitchen came the rattle of dishes in water and the opening and closing of cabinets as Ramona put away the dinner things. "He probably got his jollies from little boys. He sure fooled me, though. I used to think I could smell a narc a mile away. *Hombre,* I been warned by *el bueno Dios,* and as soon as we get enough bread together, that's it." He cocked his head at something that Wager didn't hear but that Farnsworth—familiar with the noises and silences that surrounded his cabin—knew. "That sounds like them now." A moment or two later, the German shepherd that roamed the yard around the small house began a deep bark. "Yeah, that's them—up we go, Chico!" He handed the sleepy bundle of rubbery arms and fuzzy-warm pajamas to Wager. "Hold him a minute while I lock up the dog."

It had taken Wager another month to ride this far on Bruce the Juice's coattails; he had shaken hands first with one, then another, and then another dealer—or "businessman," as the Juice liked to call them. As always, they had kept that distance and caution of dealers who had enough trusted buyers so that they did not have to take chances. But Wager had not pushed;

85

he moved slowly and kept Bruce's account fat. After a while, he had a chair of his own at the Timber Line, and finally he had met Farnsworth.

"Hey, Farns—this here's Gabe. I told you about him!" Bruce tried to sound cool, but Wager, half standing to shake hands with Farnsworth, heard excitement in the Juice's voice. "Sit down, man! You still on that Mexican beer kick?"

Farnsworth's eyes were dimly visible in the bar's low light. He kept them on Wager. "Tecate."

"I'll get it for you, man. Sit down! I'll be right back."

"Bruce says you're his best buyer."

"He sells good stuff. I appreciate that."

"How's his price?"

Wager shrugged. "The Juice is fair. But, like anybody else, I'm always looking for a better deal. You onto any?"

"Maybe, maybe not. It depends on the market at the time."

"It depends on how many middlemen there are, too."

"What makes you think he's not the source?"

"The way he hopped up when you came in? *Mierda, hombre!* He's a good kid and he's on the make, but he doesn't have the"—Wager groped for the word with his hands—"seriousness of somebody at the top. We say he *no tiene huevos.*"

For the first time, Farnsworth smiled, the cheeks clenching slightly above the line of his beard. He reached deep into one of the baggy pockets of his army field jacket and pulled out a huge yellow pipe that reminded Wager of the Sherlock Holmes movies. "I've got some friends who might cut your overhead."

Bruce came back with the Mexican beer; his eyes flicked first at Farnsworth, then at Wager. "You guys getting it together O.K.?"

"Sure, Juice." Farnsworth smiled and nodded thanks for the beer. "*Salud y pesos.*"

"*Mucho de ambos,*" answered Wager, and Farnsworth laughed.

"What's that mean, man?" The Juice twisted a lime slice

into his own fresh drink that blossomed at the top with green leaves, toothpicks, straws, and a crescent of orange.

"Just a saying," Wager said, smiling, "like good luck."

"Oh." The eyes flicked again and Bruce sucked at the glass.

After a few minutes, Farnsworth drained his beer. "I better cut—Ramona's got supper going."

"Don't rush off, man." Bruce's enthusiasm sounded forced.

"Give me a call sometime, Gabe. The number's in the book."

*"Por supuesto."*

Bruce watched Farnsworth go out through the double entry into the darkening street. He stared at his glass in silence for a while, then looked up. "Did he lay a deal on you?"

Wager sipped his beer. "He said he might be able to cut my overhead."

"Shit." The Juice twirled the glass in its puddle of melted frost. "You're the best customer I got. And you're between me and the street, too. If you go over to him, I got to go back on the street, and man that's a bad scene."

"Business is business, Juice. Besides, you told me you got along real sweet up here—no competition."

"Well, yeah, we cover for each other every now and then. But to buy out a guy's best customer! It's like he lets me have a customer long enough to see if he's legitimate; then he moves in and cuts me out. I'll bet he'll charge you more than he charges me, but less than I got to charge you to make my profit. That way he can raise his prices. It's dingy shit, you know?"

"I'm not in this for my health. He gave me a chance to raise my profit margin. I'll see what he offers. Business is business, Juice, and I want to get off the street, too."

"He's my supplier—I can't get underneath the son of a bitch. I just think it's shit! I finally get a good steady customer and start making a little money, and I get fucking underbid. And I can't do a goddam thing about it, man. He'd cut me off and I wouldn't have nothing at all."

87

"Maybe you can come up with stuff he doesn't have."

"I get everything from him. He's the only source around. We need us a free market system, man."

The Juice was learning that it wasn't all fun and games. Wager did his best to hide the feeling of satisfaction, but something must have tinged his voice. "Well, we all got problems, brother."

Bruce looked up quickly. "I'll remember you said that."

Wager smiled broadly. "You do that."


Outside, the dog had stopped barking and in the silence now surrounding Farnsworth's cabin, Wager heard the slam of car doors and a murmur of laughter and voices. Ramona came in from the kitchen wiping her hands on a dishtowel and hung it to dry on the wire running behind the stove's hot chimney. "Here, Gabe, let me take him." She was short and her black hair had been plaited and coiled over each ear in a style that Wager had not seen for years. On her arm, just below her elbow, spread the dark red birthmark Chandler had told him about.

Wager patted the small point of the sleepy boy's shoulder and the bundle wriggled a bit heavier on his chest and sighed deeply. "He's O.K.; *no es problema.*"

"It's past his bedtime," she said with a mother's authority that, Wager thought, seemed too early a burden for a girl so small and young. But that, too, was something he remembered now; all the little girls in the old neighborhood had had short childhoods. *"Vete a la camito, Pepe."*

Wager lifted the sagging warmth to her and watched the woman carry the child into the bedroom. Two small feet dangled loosely over her arm as she closed the door behind her, leaving Wager to find his moment of stillness and with it a sense of peace at hearing the tiny going-to-bed sounds of the child, the faint snap of the stove's fire, the easy creak of the old house around him. Farnsworth had all this, and he still

88

wanted more. Wager truly could not understand the man's greed.

He was still standing when Farnsworth led three men into the room, the large police dog sneaking guiltily behind and easing toward a warm corner of the room. "Gabe, these are the other partners in our deal: Charlie, Bones, and Manny. Gabe's the dude they call Mr. Taco. He put up the last five."

"I heard about you all over." Bones stuck out a long hand knotty with fleshless joints. "People all over say you really service the street culture."

Wager touched hands with them. Flint looked puzzled until Gabe smiled and said, "I been looking at that picture you sold me."

"Oh, right—I thought you looked familiar. Perhaps not as heavy a beard, but, yes, I remember now. You've gotten something out of that photograph?"

"Sure. It's been talking to me. It's somebody standing all alone and night's coming on. It—ah—has a clear statement and good technique." He hoped that sounded like what Suzy said.

"Say, you really are onto it; that's quite a professional assessment."

"Well, you know, you just got to use your eyes."

Baca—Manny the Man—remained half a step behind the other two and studied Wager through the thick lenses of his horn-rimmed glasses. "I never heard of no Mr. Taco. Not around Nineteenth and Market in Denver, I ain't."

That was a stretch of bars with Mexican names and the peppery-sour odor Wager remembered from a trip to Juárez. "I got my own territory." Like two cats, he and Baca pretended indifference while studying the things that Anglo non-cats couldn't see. With Baca, Wager would have to be very careful.

Farnsworth brought out bottles and glasses: Wild Turkey, Pinch, Bacardi dark, and some mixes. "Sit down, folks; pleasure

89

before business—we got some tequila, too, if you want some. Jo-Jo won't be in for another hour and a half."

"You heard from him?"

"He called from just east of Denver when he stopped for gas. That was . . . when, Gabe?"

"Half-hour ago."

"He didn't have no trouble?" Manny poured rum and squeezed a lime into the glass.

"Nope." Farnsworth mixed a drink for Ramona, who came out of the bedroom closing the door lightly behind her.

"I still think it was risky," said Flint. "But we didn't really have any options, did we?"

Farnsworth shook his head. "It was his connection all the way."

"How much do you think he should get?" asked Bones.

Farnsworth's eyebrows bobbed. "Thirty percent?"

"He won't like that." Flint laughed. "I suspect Jo-Jo's thinking of a hundred percent markup."

"Fuck that," said Baca. "We gave him the capital, didn't we? And the truck. All he done was drive."

"Nevertheless, it was his contact," reminded Flint.

Farnsworth wagged his hands. "Let's not sweat it too much. If it's as good as Jo-Jo says, I'm willing to go up to forty percent markup for him. Any higher, Jo-Jo can peddle it himself."

Baca laughed for the first time. "That little shit couldn't handle that much grass. He'd get busted inside of twenty-four hours if he tried to move that much stuff."

"Manny's right." Ramona's quiet voice made the others pause, and Wager looked at her with a sharper interest. "We got the outlets; eight hundred pounds of grass is too much for Jo-Jo to handle by himself. And it's our money that put down the deal for him. I say we don't go over thirty on this first load, and then raise it with the next load."

"He's gonna squeal like a stuck hog."

"Let the little shit squeal. Who's gonna listen?" Baca turned to Gabe. "You ain't said nothing yet."

It was more challenge than question; Wager took his time answering. "We set him up in business, we gave him the bread for no interest, we handle the marketing. We owe him for his connection and for driving. Thirty sounds real fair to me." He held Baca's eyes. "It won't take much to squeeze him if he don't like it."

"We'll see." Baca wasn't going to give an inch; Wager would have to prove whatever he promised.

A little over an hour later, the dozing German shepherd in the corner raised his head with a low growl. Farnsworth held up his hand to silence the talk in the room. "I think that's him. C'mon, Rex." He opened the front door for the dog and followed it out. Wager savored the quick breath of cold air from the glassed-in front porch. In a few moments they heard the whining clatter of a Volkswagen rock up the rutted and stony road from the highway. It squeaked into the front yard and the engine died.

"Here he is, gang, Jo-Jo the dog-faced boy!"

He followed Farnsworth in, flesh pale and eyes baggy from the two-day drive. Even his Afro seemed to wilt on the ends. "Hey, people! Jesus, do I need a drink! And, man, do I have good stuff."

"Is it real Colombian?" asked Bones.

"That weed has such good fumes, it doubled my gas mileage; half the time the van's wheels weren't even on the ground!"

Farnsworth handed him a strong drink and they waited until he drained it and had another started. "Man, that's good. I didn't want to touch anything, you know, while I was driving. Do you believe a cop would shit if he stuck his head in that van to write a ticket?"

Wager laughed with the rest.

"Wow—it feels good to just sit down without that wheel.

Jesus, was there some cross wind coming across Kansas. Around them grain elevators, I could hardly keep the son of a bitch on the road." His voice died out and everyone waited. "Well? You want to see the stuff?"

They followed him into the cold night filled with every star in the sky; to the southeast, the faint glow of Nederland's few streetlights silhouetted a low ridge of shaggy mountains. The moist, pungent odor of marijuana drifted out of the van as Jo-Jo unfastened the inside panels of the vehicle's shell. The German shepherd sneezed and moved away.

"Tell me that don't smell like the real thing," said Jo-Jo, laughing.

"I'm cold," said Ramona. "I'll wait inside. Bring me a little from each bag."

Wager's eyes questioned Farnsworth.

"She's our taster," he said.

"A taster?"

"Yeah. I don't know how she does it, but if there's shit mixed with the grass, she'll spot it. She says it either tastes right or wrong, and if it tastes wrong, man, it's wrong." He opened each of the large plastic bags that had been molded between the various struts and beams of the van's body and took a pinch of the loose weed. "Be back in a minute."

"I never seen it packed loose before," said Bones. "It usually comes in bricks."

"I broke up the bricks. It rides better this way. Hell, I couldn't get no bricks into spaces like that."

Wager helped carry the slippery plastic bags into a lean-to built against the east wall of the cabin. Then they trooped back into the living room. Ramona had a dozen tiny cigarettes rolled and was sniffing at the smoke of one of them. Gabe and the others waited. She lit each one and let the fumes of the match clear before tasting, holding the smoke in her mouth but not inhaling, sniffing lightly at the column rising from the burning tip of the tiny joint. It reminded Wager of Sonnenberg and his cigars. "It's good. It's all good." With her fingers, she snuffed out the fire of the last cigarette and dumped its contents with the rest of the half-smoked grass. "If it ain't Colombian, I can't tell the difference."

"Say! What'd I tell you? Is that a contact or is that a contact? You should have seen that son of a bitch come flying onto that dirt road. That's all it was, man, just a straight dirt road between a couple of cotton fields, and that son of a bitch just set her down right on it, telephone poles and all. Ten minutes later, he was on his way south again for another load. We can get all this we want any time we want. I got a number to call—all we do is place an order, man."

"We figure you've got thirty percent coming."

Jo-Jo stared a long moment at Farnsworth. Then his sharp face darkened with blood. "Bullshit! Bullshit, I got thirty percent! It was my contact, goddam it, and my ass with it on the road. Fifty percent, and that's only fair!"

Farnsworth shrugged. "Figure it out: we put up the capital and we loaned you the vehicle."

"Perhaps it should have been spelled out more clearly," said Flint. "But I never imagined you thought of anything more than twenty or thirty percent. We need a realistic return for the kind of investment we made."

Bones added, "We put up a lot of high-risk money."

"I'll sell it myself and give you back your fucking high-risk money!"

"If you do"—Wager smiled—"I want my interest."

"What interest? Who said anything about interest?"

"I just did, *amigito*."

"Me, too," said Baca.

"You guys never said nothing about interest. You guys said it was a good deal and you wanted in on it!"

Flint fingered his red beard. "Gabe certainly has a point; it was a high-risk venture and should yield either high profit or high interest."

"Fuck you guys! You're trying to rip me off. All right, name your goddam interest. I'll pay you fuckers off and run my own operation from here on."

"Where are you gonna sell it?" asked Baca. "Where's your outlets?"

"Yeah," said Wager. "You don't want to use mine, because I don't want you to use mine. Maybe somebody else'll be more generous."

No one spoke.

"I guess not," said Wager. "What are you gonna do with all that grass? Smoke it?"

"You fuckers."

"Thirty percent this time," said Farnsworth. "The next time we'll go higher—we'll know it's not such a big risk."

"You dirty bastard!" Jo-Jo stepped forward, his thin body bent tightly by his anger. One hand started inside his shirt.

Wager said very quietly, "No," and reached behind his back.

In the silence they heard the faint whine and scratch of the German shepherd at the outer door.

Jo-Jo's pupils were tiny dots of rage as he glared at Wager. "I'll get you."

"You better do it when I'm not looking. You ain't got the balls to do it when I am."

"No heavy stuff." Ramona spoke for the first time. "We'll go thirty percent and throw in the van. Next time, it's fifty-fifty if you invest, too. Sign over the title to him, 'Cardo."

Farnsworth took the slip of paper from his wallet and filled in the blank lines on the back. He held it out to Lewis. "Take it, Jo-Jo, and let's have a drink. Hell, we should have got all this straight before."

Jo-Jo had difficulty taking his eyes off Wager; he snatched the ownership and walked stiffly to the door. "All right, fuckers. But I got ripped and I ain't forgetting." The eyes came back to Wager. "I ain't forgetting you!" He slammed the door behind him. They heard the tinny clank of the van's inside panels tossed onto the vehicle's floor and then the angry rush of the engine as Jo-Jo ground through the gears turning around in the front yard. The engine faded away in the darkness.

Farnsworth said gently, "That van cost us two thousand dollars, honey."

"If it's in his name, it can't be tied to us if he's busted on the next trip," she said.

Flint's red beard gapped in a short "Haw! 'Mona, you are sharp!"

"Wowee," breathed Bones. "For a minute there, I thought it was going to be the O.K. Corral around here. I didn't know old Jo-Jo carried iron."

"He don't. It's a hunting knife. I knew the son of a bitch was crazy, but I never thought he'd try and use it." Baca glanced at Wager. "Do you tote a piece?"

Wager did not miss the new note of respect in Baca's voice; *machismo* was the willingness to fight, or, in Baca's case, to plant bombs in parked cars. "Everybody down home carries one." Wager drew the stubby Bauer .25 from its holster where it rested on his kidney; the small square handle felt toylike in his palm. He preferred his larger gun, the Star .45, but that was too professional for what he was supposed to be.

"You ever use that thing?"

"Not unless somebody makes me," he said honestly.

"Wowee," said Bones again. "Let's all have a drink—to good ol' Jo-Jo!"

After the marijuana was divided and the others had gone, Farnsworth led Gabe back into the warmth of the living room. Ramona had gone to bed; Farnsworth tossed another log onto the low fire in the Franklin stove. The German shepherd blinked bloodshot eyes at the sound and flopped back sleepily in the corner behind the stove.

"I don't like to see that heavy stuff, Gabe."

"Sometimes there's no choice. Sometimes it's part of the job."

95

Farnsworth filled his pipe and passed the bottle to Wager, who splashed a couple of fingers of Wild Turkey into a glass. "Well, maybe Ramona and me have been lucky so far. We haven't had any of the heavy crap around here yet. I suppose if it comes, we'll move on."

And leave their mess to be cleaned up by someone else. "You must have enough money to quit. The kid's gonna start noticing things soon."

Farnsworth fiddled with the pipe, bobbing the yellow fire of the match up and down with his breath. "Yeah, we got some money stashed. But we could always use more. Ramona's got it figured that in two years, the way things are going, we'll have enough to quit and be comfortable for a long time."

"She makes the decisions?"

"Well, she's smart. Like giving Jo-Jo the van—I never would of thought of unloading that thing on him. Hell, if you really want to know, she's the one who's figured out this whole setup." He wagged his head, the loose springs of hair bobbing. "Hell, if it wasn't for her, I'd still be nickel-and-diming on the street. And little Pedro—he's going to be just as sharp. You know he's just turned five and already he's starting to read? That little son of a gun picked it up from 'Sesame Street.'"

"That's something," said Wager.

"He's a good kid. A little more money and we'll be able to give him a real good start."

Paid for by people whose start was stolen by an army of users dumping shit into their blood. "That's fine," said Wager.

"You know, this crap should be legalized. I mean coke and pot—hell, nobody gets hooked on that. And even the other stuff, people are going to get it anyway. Look what they're willing to pay now! It would wipe me out overnight if they legalized the shit; the bottom would fall right out of the market. But think of the money the government would save. I mean, people are going to do it anyway, you know? Like Ramona says, all we do is give people what they want, and they want it enough to pay what we charge. Just like Prohibition. Hell, I got a buddy whose old man made it big running rum during Prohibition, and when you think about it, that's all this is. It's the same goddam thing. You know up in Aspen no jury'll convict a dealer? The fuzz files all their cases down in Denver because nobody up there thinks it's a crime to be in this line of work. And it'll be that way in the rest of the country, too: first the legalization of marijuana, then the other stuff. It's coming because it's what the people want. We're just a little bit ahead of our time is all, and I hope legalization holds off just long enough for me to make my score."

"Me, too," said Wager.

The late-evening wind creaked the timbers of the cabin and crackled through the wooden shingles on the low roof. The flames hidden in the Franklin stove gave muffled flaps and died back. Wager sipped at the bourbon and felt again the motion build up in the room: the wind around its walls, the steady creak of the rocking chair where Farnsworth sat, the waggle of the tufts of hair. "What happened with the narc you were telling me about—Chandler?"

"What? Oh—yeah. I was telling you about that, wasn't I? Well, he set me up. I trusted the son of a bitch and he set me up for a buy and bust." Again the shake of the head. "He even fooled Ramona—she thought he was O.K."

"What happened at the bust?"

"Now there's a question."

"How's that?"

"Well, we went with the deal and then the buyer—Rietman was his name—blew the whistle, and the next thing I know I'm asshole-to-asshole with a big forty-four, and my old buddy Chandler's saying, 'Surprise, I'm a narc.'"

"But the bust didn't stick?"

"No, and that's what I can't figure"—Farnsworth aimed the pipestem at Gabe—"because there I am in the cage thinking, Shit, I just blew five years, and wondering what little Pedro would look like in 1980, when my lawyer comes in to tell me there's no case. He says the stuff I sold them was lactose."

"It wasn't?"

"Hell, no, it wasn't! Man, I lost almost forty thousand dollars' worth of coke on that deal, and all I could do was smile at that lawyer and say, 'How about that?' "

All the motion in the room froze and Wager felt himself freezing with it. "You sold Rietman the real thing?"

"Yeah, I did—I'm an honest dealer, man. You know what I bet?"

Wager knew. He knew exactly what Farnsworth bet, because he bet the same thing. But he made himself say, "What?"

"I bet either Chandler or Rietman or both of them switched it. I bet those sons of bitches just picked up that brick and rode off into the sunset with it. You and me, we're just giving the people what they want; but those sons of bitches are cheats, man! They just ain't honest!"

## 7

It was one of those late-autumn periods along the Front Range when clouds settled in for long, drizzly days. Above eight thousand feet, the mountains were getting a wet snow that would pack solidly for the winter; in Denver it rained steadily —not heavy, not light, just steady. Wager listened to the faint crackle of drops on the wide lip of the balcony outside his apartment. Down below, the normally busy street held a Sunday stillness. On this kind of wet and muffled afternoon, he wished for a fireplace or wished that Lorraine . . . He turned from the rain-speckled glass of the balcony door and clicked on the television; the excited voice of a football announcer faded into the glare of cheering voices as someone scored a Sunday-afternoon touchdown somewhere. Wager left the noise on and went into the kitchen to heat the skillet. Ed Johnston would be watching the game. He'd have to talk to Ed Johnston. And then to Sonnenberg. Best to wait until the game was over before calling. He cracked a couple of eggs onto the hot iron skillet and scraped a patty of hash browns from the half of potato wrapped in tinfoil and still generally fresh. A spoon or two of green chili as the eggs came off; toast, the pot of coffee that never tasted exactly right until it had chilled and been reheated. And the rain. His wife—ex-wife—had liked the rain: walking in it, listening to it; the dampness made her skin feel soft, she said. She had liked fireplaces, too. She did not like a cop's hours. But he had been a cop in the uniformed division when she married him, and there hadn't been any Sunday mornings at all then; Saturday night was always one long hassle, and the paperwork was never finished until well into Sunday. "I don't mind," she said at first; but she did mind, and pretty soon she couldn't hide it any more.

But before they were married, he had told her what a cop's life would be like.

Well, tried to. Maybe he hadn't told her enough. Maybe way down deep he had thought that she would get used to it and then he could have both. Maybe with himself and her, he had only been playing games. He knew for a fact he had not told her enough about the new O.C.D. job. But she had been so pretty—she still was. And there had been times when they both forgot he was a cop. A few times; and then fewer. And then none at all. And in these quiet, inward-gazing times, he could see through the surprise and shock of Lorraine's leaving to know that there were no games left to play.

He shoved his toast through the last of the chili and eggs and rinsed the dishes, then stood gazing once more through the rain-splattered balcony doors at the grayness that masked the mountains west of the city. A wet autumn promising lots of snow, bringing lots of run-off in the spring, and with it poor fishing until late in the season. Not that it made any difference to him any more; despite all the leave he had built up over the last three or four years, he knew he wouldn't take it. The mountains held quiet spells like this one, times that trapped him with echoes and memories, times when his mind kept jumping from one painful thing to another. It was better not to take leave. Better to be able to sleep through these Sundays. Best of all if he didn't have to call Johnston.

He waited until the game ended and the sports announcer was explaining the holes in the Bronco pass defense to another sports expert, who kept saying, "Yes, Don, but you have to give credit to . . ." He turned it off and telephoned Johnston.

"Hello?" Behind the sergeant's voice, he heard, "Yes, Don, and you have to give credit to . . ."

"This is Gabe, Ed."

"What's the problem?" There had to be a problem; Wager never called him at home unless there was one.

"It's the Rietman bust. Last night Farnsworth told me he sold Rietman the real stuff."

In the background, the sports expert had begun to tell Don about next week's match against Oakland. "Jesus Christ."

Wager waited.

"Jesus goddamn Christ!"

"I guess you want a report in writing?"

"Yes—no! Have you told anybody else? S.I.B?"

"Hell, no."

"O.K., Gabe—don't get pissed. Just let me think a minute."

He knew what the results of Ed's thought would be.

"I better call the inspector. I'll get back to you. You at home?"

"Yes."

The gray became darker. Wager left the lights off and sat and read through his small notebook until it became too dim to see. At some point, evening slid into night before the telephone rang again. It was Sonnenberg himself. "Can you come down to the office, Gabe?"

"Yes, sir."

He lived closer than either Ed or the inspector; only the

stairway light and the duty watch's room glowed from the windows in the painted brick wall that faced the O.C.D. parking lot. He sat at his desk and waited. In a little while, the door warning rattled loudly and Wager recognized the inspector's steady stride thumping the bare wooden floor.

"Let's wait in my office. Ed will be here in a few minutes."

Sonnenberg was in the middle of his ritual of lighting a cigar when the door buzzed again and Ed's hurrying footsteps echoed through the empty desks and partitions. The duty watch finally roused and poked his head around a corner to see who was making all the commotion. "Oh, hi, Sergeant Johnston."

"Evening, Tom."

Ed rapped at the doorframe and came in, closing the door after him.

"So Farnsworth claims he sold cocaine and not lactose," said Sonnenberg as soon as the sergeant sat down.

"Yes, sir."

"Could he be leading you on?"

"I don't think so. I hope not. If he was, it means he thinks I'm a narc or a snitch. I'm sure he doesn't think that."

"Maybe he was just drawing the long bow."

Wager blinked; he hadn't heard that phrase in years. Every now and then, Sonnenberg came up with something like that. "He didn't seem to be, sir."

Johnston—rocking first on one ham, then on the other as the wooden captain's chair grew harder against his thin body —asked Wager, "Any chance of his trying to frame Rietman and Chandler for revenge, maybe?"

"Only if he thinks I'm a narc or a snitch. Only if he thinks I'll carry his story to authorities, Ed."

"Oh, yeah. You said."

"Possibly he's just testing you with a false story?" asked Sonnenberg.

"That could be." But Wager didn't think so. Farnsworth's surprise and wry humor seemed genuine. "He'd sure know where the story came from if word ever got out about Rietman."

One, two, three heavy yellow smoke rings bounced gently off the green blotter on Sonnenberg's desk and drew into a quivering column over the desk lamp. "Yes," said the inspector slowly, "yes, he would know for certain. And we don't know for certain that Rietman was alone in this. We don't know if he's working with someone else in this unit or in D.P.D."

"Jesus," said Johnston, "if the guys in the department start looking out of the corners of their eyes at each other, we might as well hang up our jocks."

One more smoke ring. "And we've invested an awful lot of time and money on Farnsworth. Too much to risk it now. All right, what we do is this: we sit on the Rietman thing until we nail Farnsworth. We don't move on Rietman at all."

"Yes, sir."

"Maybe it was Chandler," said Johnston. "Maybe I should check with D.E.A. and see what's in Chandler's history."

Sonnenberg shook his head. "They'd want to know why you're asking. I don't want to risk a leak until we've got Farnsworth."

"It wasn't Chandler," said Wager.

Johnston and Sonnenberg looked at him.

He took out the small notebook. Turning to a dog-eared page, he read the summary of his telephone conversation with Chandler, emphasizing that the D.E.A. man and Rietman had driven alone in separate cars back to headquarters after the bust, and that the dope had been in Rietman's possession all the way.

"Maybe Chandler lied?"

"No," said the inspector. "It would be too easy to verify. The surveillance team would know who drove what."

"And Rietman signed the stuff into the custodian's office. He was the only one in the chain of possession from the bust to the locker."

"And he's had four months to sell that cocaine."

"I can check out his recent behavior," said Johnston. "If he's spending more than he's making, we can find out easy enough without tipping anybody."

"I suppose we can go that far. But for God's sake, don't make waves."

"Yes, sir."

Sonnenberg's cigar crackled gently. "Gabe, put all this in writing as soon as you can—for Ed's eyes and mine only. No one else, not even Suzy. There's not a blessed thing we can do until we bag Farnsworth; but when he's out of the way . . ."

"Then we'll sack that son of a bitch Rietman."

In his mind, Wager corrected the sergeant. First they would sack the facts. And then Rietman. So it would stick on the bastard.

Wager drew routine surveillance until late in the week, which was fine with him. Since he was supposed to be peddling 150 pounds of the choicest Colombian weed, he had to stay out of Nederland anyway; and at least surveillance got him away from the small apartment. But it did not stop him from thinking about Rietman. Or from feeling the anger well up in his stomach with a sour taste that made the lukewarm coffee churn uneasily in his gullet. Things like that did happen— Hansen had said it months ago. But you did not expect it to happen in your own unit. You didn't expect it with someone you had trusted. *Caga*—you never really expected it. What you did expect was that cops would do their jobs, nothing more or less. You expected more from the men who worked with you than you did from a marriage.

His suspect, a slender Negro male in his early twenties, came out of the dark apartment building. He stood a moment or two on his yellow high heels to case the street, then with a loose, cocky walk went east toward Emerson Avenue. Wager, slumped against the shadow of the car seat, emptied his cup of coffee back into the thermos and marked the time on a contact card: 1:23 A.M. The suspect's gray topcoat flickered briefly in the barred shadows of treeless limbs before turning north out of sight on the empty avenue. Wager waited two or three minutes, then swung after the figure, expecting—and finding—that the suspect's car, which he had earlier parked at a distance from the apartment, was gone. He noted that on the card and, with a yawn, started home; routine periodic surveillance for bits and pieces of this and that. In the morning, he would give his cards to Suzy, who would give them to Ashcroft. And they might build into something now or later. Or they might not. That was what routine surveillance meant.

He turned up the volume on the radio pack under the seat and half listened to the quiet traffic of District 2 while his mind kept sliding back to Rietman. Thank God Rietman was new to the unit and did not have wide exposure among the snitches. When the word got out about him, all those he touched would either be terrified that Rietman might have sold them for a deal or would be twice as hard to squeeze because Rietman proved that cops were no different from crooks. That son of a bitch; when the story finally hit the street, it would hurt everybody and everything. It would erode the power that Wager and other cops had worked at so hard to give weight to their promises and threats; worst of all, it would raise a question in every cop's mind—as if there weren't enough worries already. A rogue cop. A crooked cop. It had really happened, and to him.

He eased up on the gas pedal, which his anger had pressed. Evidence. It was all circumstantial, and without an admission from Farnsworth that he had sold Rietman cocaine, there would be no conviction. The inspector was right: the only way they could get to Rietman was through Farnsworth, and the only way Farnsworth would admit to selling to Rietman would be if he was afraid of something bigger. Wager could see it coming: pop Farnsworth so hard that there would be a deal. Sonnenberg—and himself, too, he guessed—would put more value on hanging Rietman than Farnsworth. But both of the bastards should hang; it was just that Rietman should have more air under his feet. He pulled into the numbered parking place behind his apartment and disconnected the radio pack, clipping it onto his belt. Perhaps there was another way to cook bacon: if Rietman thought Farnsworth was about to be popped, maybe he would want to beat Farnsworth in copping a plea. Maybe there were two roads to the same place.

He called D.P.D. at midmorning; Rietman and his partner were on patrol in District 1. Wager arranged to meet them on their coffee break at a Jack-in-the-Box drive-in.

Rietman was riding shotgun; his partner looked across at Wager curiously. "Is that you underneath the beard, Wager?" Rietman asked. "What do you want now?"

"A few questions about Farnsworth. Why don't you get in my car? Your partner can monitor the radio."

Rietman strode slowly to Wager's vehicle and slid in beside him. "I hope it's worth your fucking up my coffee break."

Wager kept his eyes to the front of the car where a waitress trotted back and forth carrying trays up and down the long row of covered parking slots. "We're real close to busting Farns-worth."

"Gee, that's nice."

"When we get him, he may want to bargain."

"So let the son of a bitch. He ain't my worry no more."

Wager ordered a hamburger and coffee. Rietman did not want anything. "If he bargains, he'll confess to everything he's ever done so we can't charge him on anything additional later."

"What's your thing, Wager? What are you laying on me?"

He was cool. Wager smiled and couldn't help a touch of sour admiration: Rietman was one cool dude and a good actor.

"We'll be looking at all his deals—everything he ever did."

"And?"

"I might want to check some of his story with you."

"As long as it's during working hours. Anything extra's time and a half."

He gave Rietman a few minutes' silence, a few minutes to think—to say something more. But the uniformed cop was quiet.

"Well, I thought you'd like to know that we're real close to getting him."

"Detective Wager, sir, I just don't give one small shit one way or another."

On his way to O.C.D. headquarters, Gabe ran the scene through his memory over and over, seeking something in the words or voice or eyes that told him Rietman was indeed worried. But nothing showed. Either Rietman was one of the smoothest liars Wager had ever run across or he really wasn't worried. And if Rietman wasn't, Wager should be—because something was wrong.

He rapped on Johnston's doorframe; the Sergeant looked up from the sports section of the *Post.* "Gabe—come on in. Did you hear about the MDA case? The one in the Springs?"

"No."

"Three to five! They're appealing, but it won't get nowhere."

"I thought we had them on a class-three felony."

"Yeah; well, the Springs D.A. offered them a deal."

"I see. What about Rietman? Did you get anything yet?" Johnston had started following the paper trails that Rietman, like everyone else, left through a community.

Ed said, "Score, zip. If he has a second bank account, it's either in another name or not around his neighborhood."

"He wouldn't use a bank near home. He knows our procedures."

"And his charge accounts are routine, no big purchases. I

found nothing unusual in his spending habits. But we won't have access to his tax files until sometime next spring."

"Any recent trips?"

"Not that we could find out. So far, he's Mr. Clean."

"Or Mr. Smooth."

"He probably stashed the stuff until it cools off. He's under no pressure to sell it."

"Maybe." And maybe not. Motive: money. Who needs money? People who want things or who are in debt. Rietman didn't seem to want anything. "Did you check his credit rating? Has he made any early payments?"

"Nope. And he's never missed a payment. Besides, that would be in his official file."

True enough; officers in debt were officers in trouble. "Medical expenses? Girl friend?"

Johnston shook his head. "There's no indication he's ever been caught offsides in his life."

"Just one."

"Yeah. One."

It really didn't fit, and the rough edges irritated Wager's mind. Yet why would Farnsworth lie unless he was testing Wager? And why should he test him even after Wager had been let in to the dealing? "Do you have a list of Rietman's old snitches?"

"What for?"

"If he hasn't moved that junk yet, he's going to sooner or later. And he's sure as hell not going on the street himself."

"You mean he might be using one of his snitches to market it?"

"He has to do it somehow."

"You're right." Johnston unlocked one of the long drawers of a filing cabinet. "Yeah—they're here." He stopped and looked up at Wager. "But the inspector said he didn't want to do anything until after we've had a shot at Farnsworth."

"Who's doing anything? We just want to know if any of the

snitches are in fat city all of a sudden."

"Oh. I guess that'd be O.K." He handed Wager the file. "He didn't have time to build up much of a stable."

Gabe copied the three entries and their telephone numbers. The first, Louis's, he thought sounded familiar. The other two were new: Paddy-O and Ritchie. "Anybody working these people now?"

"Not in our squad." Ed ran his fingers through the thinning red hair. "You know, Gabe, I don't know . . ."

"Do I know you don't know what?"

"I don't know if you should even ask around about these C.I.s. You got too much yardage to lose right now."

"If he hasn't moved that junk yet, we've still got a chance to catch it. Or if he's doing it now, we can stop it. Or if he's already done it, his middleman might be thinking of leaving town. Besides, I want that son of a bitch a hell of a lot more than I want Farnsworth."

"Me, too, Gabe. But the inspector says something else. Nope—you stay off these guys. I'll check with the inspector when he gets in. In the meantime, just don't even go near these guys."

Without a *duces tecum* subpoena, Wager couldn't go through the telephone company's records for the addresses of the snitches' numbers; without the sergeant's approval, he couldn't get the *duces tecum.* Gabe smiled. *"Bueno*—I'll just sit *con mis manos en el seno."*

Or almost with his hands in his lap; at his desk, he dialed Fat Willy's office number.

The bartender answered as usual when Wager asked if Fat Willy was there. "Maybe he is, maybe he ain't. Who wants him?"

"Gabe."

"I'll ask around."

A moment later, Fat Willy breathed heavily at his ear: "I was feeling maybe you was a dead greaser by now."

"It's nice to know you've been thinking of me, Willy. How are you and Hansen getting along?"

"We gets along. You want to know about my health and love life, too?"

"I know you've got a lot of both—and they're going to last a long time because you are going to help me out."

"Sure, baby! You cut me off, and that's the way it stays."

"Business is business, Willy. Don't take it personal. Now listen up, I got something I want you to do."

"I ain't listening. And I ain't doing."

"And you ain't going to get any action when Hansen turns your jacket back over to me."

The black's voice dropped so that only an angry rumble came through the earpiece. "This nigger ain't working for no spics no more." The line clicked dead.

Wager went down the list to the next number. Again it was answered by a female voice he did not recognize. "Is Doc there?"

"Who're you?"

"Gabe."

"Just a minute."

"Gabe, baby! Long time no! Hey, where you been, man? Hey, baby, I really been swinging since you been away."

"That's fine, Doc. Listen, there's something I want you to do."

"Sure, man—any time. Hey, this Hansen cat's all right. He don't miss nothing. You put me on a good man, baby."

"Doc—listen up."

"I am! That's what I'm doing, man. Lay it on me: I'm all ears."

"I want you to find out who's been heavy in coke in the last four months."

The line was silent. Doc wasn't all jive turkey. "Funny you should ask."

"Why?"

"There's been a lot of snort around. Good stuff, too, but it's thinning out now."

"Around since when?"

"Since this fall!"

"Any names?"

"Just a minute." A palm clamped down over Doc's mouthpiece for a moment. "O.K., Wager—I sent the ginch for a pack of cigarettes. What she don't know, she can't say, can she?"

"Names, Doc."

"Names. There's a bunch of new ones—people gonna sell what people want to buy. But there's one I heard about who's supposed to be really big."

"Well?"

"Well, I ain't heard that he deals in coke, but the word is he can get anything anybody wants. And all they want."

"The name, Doc."

"That's what I'm trying to tell you—it's Mr. Taco."

"Jesus Christ."

"Well, can I help it if that's his name? So he's a Chicano or something. They do a little dealing, you know. His name's all over the street and he's really big. I tipped Hansen on it but he ain't come up with nothing yet."

"I'll let Hansen handle it, then. Any other names?"

"It's got to be coke?"

"And within the last four months."

Another silence. "No. Not just coke and not just in the last four months. I can't think of nobody that fits that."

"How about Louis, Paddy-O, or Ritchie?"

"What Louis? There's three or four Louises around. Paddy-O's a dude come in six, eight months ago. He's small shit. He ain't handling nothing but a little grass. He's one of these guys that thinks he's bigger than he is, you know?"

"I know."

"Ritchie—I know a couple Ritchies, too, but none tied in with coke."

"Do you have phone numbers for your Louises or Ritchies?"

"Yeah, a couple. You want them? Hang on."

Doc's voice came back, "Here's the Louises: 394–7198, 727–6365. Ritchie's is 355–3735."

"That second one, what Louis is that?"

"That's Louis Sloane. But he ain't much of nothing, neither."

Sloane, Louis. Wager now remembered the small-time hustler: white male, mid-thirties, a little dope, a stable of a couple of whores, a habit to support. "No sudden spending? No wheeling around?"

"Sloane? Shit, no! He's hustling anything he can get a line on, and he's so goddam hungry it's even funny to watch him boogie. Naw, he ain't into anything big. Hell, he uses almost everything he gets. That's why he can't get ahead."

"One more thing, Doc."

"Lay it on me."

"Don't tell anyone I've been asking. Keep it just between you and me."

"Not even Hansen?"

"No one."

"That sounds like something heavy going down."

"It could be. If you hear anything about coke in the last four months, give me a call at the O.C.D. It's a lot of coke—if you're in on it, you can make yourself a bundle. But it's got to be with me only."

"Hey, baby, cool, and I hear you."

Wager tried several more numbers from the little book of informants' coded addresses. The answers were the same: there was more cocaine around, but none of the C.I.s knew anyone who had recently unloaded a large quantity of it. A mysterious dealer may be handling it—this Mr. Taco—but the C.I.s did not know much more about him than the name.

Wager sat at his desk in silence and stared across the shallow bowl of the city toward the distant ranges of peaks. Apparently, Rietman hadn't sold off the stuff in big lots. And he had not made any trips, either. And he wasn't spending. Neither were his snitches—though Wager would like to see for himself just to be sure. The cocaine that was on the street didn't seem to come from him. So it must be stashed somewhere, Rietman just forgetting about it until it was absolutely safe to bring it out. And why not? It was as good as money in the bank—better, in fact, since its value went up with inflation instead of down. And that would fit with what Wager was beginning to see as Rietman's character: self-controlled, methodical, far-sighted, patient. He could have been a God damned good cop.

Suzy stood at his elbow and cleared her throat. Wager, pulled out of thought, looked up with surprise.

"Would you—ah—think you might want to see some of my shots?"

"Shots?" It took a moment or two before he remembered. "Photographs! Sure, *por supuesto*, Suzy. You have some here?"

She placed an official manila folder on his desk and opened it. "There are a few I took." Her voice was shy. "They're not, you know, great, but I like them."

Wager looked through the black-and-white pictures. Half a dozen were of birds ("That's my parakeet") and dogs ("That's my dog, Herman"), and the rest were street scenes: corners with a single blurred figure striding quickly out of sight, bus stops with three or four people slouching apart and staring blankly away from each other, a streetlamp showing an empty pool of gray light against solid black. They all said "lonely," and Wager did not want to see what they said. Loneliness was the sea everyone swam in; he did not need these pictures to tell him that. And it was depressing to see one so young as Suzy already learning it. Somehow it seemed she should have been spared that knowledge for a while. "Those are real nice pictures, Suzy. You've got a real talent."

Her face reddened as she quickly gathered the photographs together. "It's fun—it's something to do."

"Well, they really are nice."

Sergeant Johnston strode from the inspector's office. "Gabe? On those snitches we were talking about, the inspector says absolutely not. We lay off until you-know-who is in the bag."

Wager stretched and pushed away from his desk. "Then I guess I'd better get back up to Nederland."

# 8

For a week, Wager's hints and nudges were ignored by Farnsworth; Chandler had burned the man shy of dealing with anyone new, even with Gabriel Villanueva.

"I have this *amigo*," Gabe told Ramona, "who can get a pilot and an airplane any time we need it. And the guy's flown the border half a dozen times."

She curled her legs up on the cowhide couch and sipped at a cup of coffee. In the cabin's steamy bathroom, Peter splashed and wheezed a rubber duck.

"So now you can have your own business?"

"I wish it was that easy. This kind of deal takes a hell of a lot more bread than I got. He's not going to fly unless it's really worth his time."

"Like how much?"

"A lot of K's. The pilot wants insurance in case he goes down

—he wants fifty thousand in escrow, and then you have to add the cost of the dope and the operation to that."

"That could go as high as a hundred, maybe a hundred and fifty thousand!"

"Well, the fifty comes back after the flight. But it's still a hell of a lot bigger than I can handle by myself."

Farnsworth kicked open the door and dumped a load of firewood in the corner. "Goddam—the frost is on the pumpkin tonight!" He held his red fingers to the shimmering Franklin stove. "Did Gabe tell you about the airplane?"

"He's telling me. *¿Qué piensas tú?*"

"How's our cash reserve?"

"We could handle it O.K.," said Ramona. "But I don't know if we should. Maybe after we've seen this pilot make a run."

Farnsworth combed a flake of bark out of his wiry hair and flipped it at the dog stretched behind the stove. "Yeah. After that Chandler thing, I'd just as soon keep a low profile."

"*¡Ya lo creo!*" Wager said. "But it's a real good deal, and once I turned over my share of the load and opened a new cash flow, I'd take the other stuff off your hands. You wouldn't have to tie up your money for more than a week or so."

Ramona sipped her coffee; Farnsworth kneaded his fingers together and popped open a bottle of Tecate beer. "It sounds good"—he shook his head—"but things have been cool so far. Maybe it's better if I just stick to what I'm doing."

"Sure," said Wager. "It was just an idea." The son of a bitch.

"Maybe Baca and Flint will go in with you. Ask Manny when he gets here."

"Flint's hot to buy his art store in Taos; he won't want to risk nothing now. And Baca won't have enough by himself. Hell, there's no rush—that airplane's good any time. If you change your mind, just let me know."

"I don't think I want any of it, Gabe. But thanks for the

offer, man—I mean that." He cocked an ear toward the door. "That sounds like Manny's van now." The dog grunted awake and plodded to the door, nails scratching on the wooden floor. From the distance came the grinding lurch of a vehicle threading the rutted road. In a few minutes, a metal door clapped to and the dog slowly wagged his tail.

"Manolo! ¿Qué tal?" Farnsworth held open the inner door.

"Bien—hace mucho frio. You think we'll get a little nieve? Hi, Ramona—Gabe." He unwrapped from his sheepskin coat and leaned toward the stove. "Those your new wheels out there? And hey, dig those new shit-kickers! Man, you're coming on like a real chulo!"

Wager smiled and stretched the new tooled boots in front of him. They fit even worse than the old ones, but he was supposed to be making money. "Business has been good."

"What'd the car set you back?"

"Three and a half. But if you can't enjoy the profits, what good's the capitalist system?"

"Right on, hermano." Baca stepped aside to let Ramona haul Pedro from the bath to a place near the dry heat of the stove where she rubbed him pink with a large towel.

"Say, you guys read about that son of a bitch down in Brownsville shooting them braceros?"

Manny's van flew the red-and-black Aztec eagle flag of the United Farmworkers' Union; Wager had often wondered if Baca ever met a bracero.

"The law won't hassle that bastard," said Farnsworth. "His taxes pay that sheriff. And the braceros don't make enough to pay taxes."

Baca snorted. "I bet I couldn't take a piss in that county without getting busted for littering. Goddam pigs! What do you think, Gabe?"

"Goddam pigs."

"I'd like to plant a bomba under that son of a bitch. He wouldn't shoot no more of the brothers!"

It promised to be another full evening of sparkling political analysis. Wager hoisted Peter to his shoulders and bounced the child around the living room before tossing him giggling onto the bed where Ramona tucked him in. When the light was out, Wager poured himself a beer and settled down for Baca's lecture. Tonight it was the endurance of La Raza, because their blood was pure and their hearts were clean and God and gravity were on their side, and all Chicanos were brothers in the movement, and if the law had to be violated why shouldn't it be, because that law had been used against the people instead of for them.

Wager tried to hide his yawn as he nodded agreement; he had heard it, he had heard it all. And there was some truth in it. But when the honest things that people felt were said by Baca's mouth, those things grew dirty; Baca's speeches rode on real hurts like an insult on pain.

The lecture lasted until past midnight, Ramona as usual listening instead of talking; Farnsworth agreeing more and more vehemently with every beer; Manny Baca's voice building up into a familiar rhythm that made Wager suspect that he was using the three of them as a practice audience.

"You tell me, Gabe, if you and some Anglo go for the same job, you know who'll get it, right?"

"White skin, step right in," said Wager.

"That's right! And qualifications don't mean nothing!"

Wager knew these things that Baca fouled with his words; he had seen them a hell of a lot longer than this kid, had lived them, too: the obvious ones of lowest pay and first fired; the less obvious ones of sudden embarrassed smiles and quick silences; of unconsidered phrases, "Why don't you handle it, Gabe? You're their kind—you know them better than we do." And Wager had passed the sergeant's examination; but so had a lot of Anglos, and many of them went up while he was still a detective. If he let himself, he could find a label for it. But what counted most for him was not how the Anglo world or the Hispano world looked at him, but how he looked at himself. It was the job he did and knew he did well that was worth more than righting the ancient wrongs against Aztlan or wallowing in the complaints of pimply-faced kids who had not yet lived long enough to know what real pain was. A man did his job to his own standards without blaming Anglos or Chicanos or Spaniards or anybody else if he couldn't do the work.

"Those Spaniards, they came and conquered our civilization —they killed off the old gods and brought a new one that demanded the sacrifice not of just one man but the whole people. They brought death and famine where we had peace and plenty; they made slaves out of princes!"

Wager smiled at the thought of Manny the Aztec prince. Crap. Manny would have been just like Wager, another Aztec peon, cow dung in his ears and his forehead kissing the dirt whenever a real prince went by. But Manny would never see that. Manny was a deposed prince. Manny was his people's savior. Let my people go—I, Manuel Baca, tell you this, world! Wager forced his neck to bend agreement.

"And then the Anglos! What they couldn't steal, they cheated us out of. And they're still doing it. If you don't believe it, just try to borrow money, just try to get a job that's got some responsibility to it, man! They want cheap labor because cheap sweat means more profit—and that's the only prayer their gods know: profit! The Anglos brought their own gods, Pepsicoátl and Cocacoátl, and their prayer is profit!"

Farnsworth laughed. "That's good—Pepsicoátl and Cocacoátl."

Wager had thought it was funny the first time he heard it, too.

"Manolo—*hermano*—you know I'm as much La Raza as you or Gabe. In spirit, anyway. And there's a lot of us. It's time, man; it's time to do things!"

"That's what I keep telling people, but nobody listens. The time is now, and if we don't get our act together and do it, there ain't nobody going to do it for us."

"Well, we got money. And in this shitty country when you got money you got power. We *can* do something!"

Baca gazed through the cabin wall at some grand vision. "By God, we could set up a deal!"

"Like what?"

"Like, I know this *hombre* in the People's Labor Party. And he'll pay two, three times the price for guns delivered in Mexico."

"What kind?"

"Pistols, rifles—large-caliber stuff. Military stuff. Hell, down south, everybody wants guns. It's like they're getting ready for a war."

"Everybody?"

"Sure—you got the *bandidos* who want guns so they can move in on the big dope honchos. The big guys want guns so they can keep the *bandidos* from moving in. Both of them want guns against the *federales* and the army. The growers got to protect their fields, the transporters got to guard the stashes and the convoys. They're just hungry for weapons and there's not enough to go around."

"What side's this People's Labor Party on?"

"That's a whole different trip. They're politicos. They got people on both sides of the border, and they work with the braceros who come across. They make sure nobody gets ripped off, that kind of thing. They're all right—real caballeros."

"What do they want guns for?"

"Power! From the end of a gun, man. Suppose that son of a bitch in Brownsville was shooting at some of the People's Labor Party. Well, they get guns, they come back and wipe that mother out, and nobody around there fucks no more with the people, man!"

"Why can't they get their own guns?" asked Ramona. "They're U.S. citizens, too."

"Everybody knows them—the F.B.I.'s got a file from here

to Washington, D.C., and they can't even pick their nose without somebody finking on them. And if they tried to cross the border, the *federales* would be on them in no time."

"Why?" asked Wager.

"They been screwing around in local politics down south. Hell, you can't help getting hung up if you got any political awareness at all. The *caciques* don't want no organization of the braceros on their side of the border, either. And they own the local cops. What is it about cops, they always got to be owned instead of doing their job?"

"I still don't see what they want with guns," said Ramona. "Or how they're going to pay for them."

"That's my deal! They don't even need money. What they do is pay in dope, see? They got so many contacts down south they can get all the dope they want. What happens is we trade our money for guns, then the guns for their dope, then the dope for more money. We get a little profit on each trade, and at the same time we're helping the *hermanos* in their struggle for justice!"

Wager was always surprised at how many of the really important things came as casually as a cloud across the sun. A gentle shift of light, a new shadow on the face he had been watching, a tiny quiver: suddenly came the realization that the important thing was happening, almost without his knowledge or help, and all he had to do was let it move. Under Manny Baca's excited words, he could even hear his grandmother's voice, worn calm and level with experience and trust: *"Lo que no se hace en un año, se hace en un rato."* A moment may bring what a year hasn't.

Ramona shook her head. *"Muy malo*—too much risk. Too many people you got to work with."

"Maybe, maybe not," said Wager.

Baca looked at him, *"¿Por qué?"*

"I've been trying to tell Ramona—I can get an airplane. And one of my contacts just might have a lead on some hardware."

And won't Sergeant Johnston crap at that news. "With an airplane, we can deliver direct and cut out a lot of risk."

"Hey, that's real good!"

Wager caught the slight effort behind the words; Baca was pulling back. "We can help our *hermanos* in their struggle and help ourselves, too," reminded Gabe.

"I don't like it." Ramona frowned.

Farnsworth looked from her to Gabe to Baca. "It might really help our people, honey."

Wager held Baca's eyes in challenge. "If you really want this —if you ain't just bullshitting—we can do it."

"Who's bullshitting?"

"Some people drink a little and talk a lot. You know how it goes."

"No, I don't know how it goes. You tell me how it goes."

"Hey, *hombres*"—Farnsworth made pushing motions at the floor—"let's keep it cool. We don't need this *macho* stuff around here."

"Sure," said Wager. "Nice and cool. But *ya tengo colmillos*" —he tapped his eyetooth with a fingernail—"and I've heard people talk before. A little of it was real and a lot of it wasn't."

"Yeah? Yeah? You talk to that contact of yours. You see if he can come up with some iron. We'll see who's just talking!"

Wager sipped at his beer, "Even if I can find the guns, buying them's going to take *mucho dinero*. Maybe we'd better forget the whole thing."

Baca's face got that cross between a glare and a smile that comes when somebody has someone down and is sticking him. "What's the matter? You been talking big and want to pull out now? You find them guns, Villanueva. Dick's with me. We can come up with the coin if you can come up with the guns."

"I don't like this," said Ramona.

"It's O.K., honey. Manolo's got a good idea. We can help our people and make a little bread, too."

With help like that, the people didn't need enemies; yawning and stretching to hide his excitement, Wager stood to leave. He shook hands and paused in the doorway to smile into Baca's eyes. *"Para siempre, su servidor,"* he said.

"You want to run guns to Mexico?" Sergeant Johnston's eyes bulged slightly.

"It happens every day, Ed."

"Not by us it don't! You can't get us into something like that!"

"Let's see what Sonnenberg says."

"Let's see!"

At first the inspector said nothing, letting Wager sketch in the background without interruption. But Gabe noticed that he fiddled more than usual with his cigar. "Who brought up the idea?"

"Baca, sir."

"Did you lead Farnsworth to it in any way?"

"No, sir." The inspector was considering entrapment, something that had been in the back of Gabe's mind, too, and that Sonnenberg should have known Wager would consider. "But I sure as hell didn't shut Baca up. I think it's the only way Farnsworth's going to deal."

Sonnenberg gently touched a curl of cigar ash. "And it's him we want, not Baca."

"But, Inspector, you ain't really going to—"

"I'm just turning over the possibilities, Sergeant."

Wager waited. It wasn't his decision. The pay was the same either way. Still, he hoped to hell Sonnenberg didn't throw away all his work.

"If we even ran a water pistol down there, we'd be in trouble," Sonnenberg said.

"Oh, God, Inspector—don't even think of it!"

"It wouldn't do any good, anyway, because our jurisdiction stops at the state line." Sonnenberg drew once more on the cigar. "D.E.A. could do it; we couldn't. But D.E.A. turned him over to us, and with this Rietman thing in the air, *I* want Farnsworth." The thought trailed off in a puff of smoke.

"And if it ever turned out that we were providing guns for Farnsworth to buy dope so we could arrest him for selling that dope"—Wager smiled at the thought—"well, there would be some tight jaws in high places."

"Oh, Jesus and Mary," Johnston said.

"Gabe, there has to be some way for us to buy the dope from Farnsworth without getting involved in either guns or financing. But the way Baca wants to do it, I don't see any possibilities."

"What about front dope?" Wager asked.

"Explain."

"Suppose our gun merchant doesn't want cash. Suppose he's greedy and wants only dope instead."

His blue eyes narrowing in thought, the inspector rolled the wet tip of his cigar against his lips. Wager wondered if he slept with one. "So we would tell Farnsworth that the guns were his for a couple of kilos, and then pop him when he paid?"

"That's it. But we'll have to flash some guns. He's too paranoid just to take my word."

"We could do that all right. I think I could borrow the weapons for that."

"And I'd need someone to play the gun dealer."

The inspector nodded again. "But he'll have to be unknown: no one who's been active; no one imported. It takes paperwork to bring in a special agent, and that could warn Rietman."

That was another wrinkle. "I forgot about that."

"Someone," said Sonnenberg, "who won't talk to anyone Rietman might know."

Wager looked at Sergeant Johnston. "I think I got a man."

The cigar paused as the eyes considered.

Sergeant Johnston looked from one to the other. "Me?"

"It's a natural."

"Wait a minute, Inspector!"

"You're the only man, Ed," said Wager. "There's no way these people ever met you, and no one else has to be brought into the deal. Security would be perfect."

"Gabe's right, Sergeant. I will not risk any leaks that might warn Rietman or any confederates he may have. Besides, this whole unit is a field unit. Everyone. So you two work out the details; I'll see what I can round up in the way of weapons."

Wager made the telephone call to Nederland within the week, saying that the weapons could be bought. Farnsworth and Baca met him at the Timber Line; Ramona, who wasn't as dumb as her husband and who asked pesky questions, fortunately stayed at home.

"It wasn't my idea, Manolo. My connection says he can get weapons, but he doesn't want cash. He wants the payoff in dope."

"Well, screw him—he's trying to cut us out of our percentage on the exchange."

"I told him how you felt about it. He just said for us to get the guns somewhere else."

Baca was silent; the lenses of his glasses reflected the dim light of the room and the white streaks of snow falling beyond the tavern's small windows.

"He's got us by the balls," said Farnsworth. "We couldn't buy that many guns without a fucking license and he knows it."

"What did he show you? Did he show you any merchandise?"

"No, but he talked about dynamite stuff: M-1's, some M-16's, pistols, even a couple of rocket launchers. Three-point-six, I think he called them."

"Where in shit's he going to get stuff like that!"

Wager glanced around the almost empty room and dropped his voice. "He's in the National Guard or Army Reserve. He's a sergeant or something who can get into the armory."

"It's got to be in cash," said Baca. "I'll be goddamned if I want to give up half my profit to that bastard. A lot of that profit's supposed to go to the movement, not to that son of a bitch."

"I'll tell him the deal's off, then." Wager sat unmoving; the other two were silent also. "I kind of expected this anyway."

"Expected what?"

"That you wouldn't go through with it." Wager smiled at Baca.

"You calling me *un cobarde?*"

"I'm not calling you a goddam thing, *amigito.* All I'm saying is you told me to come up with the guns and you'd come up with the buy. I did. Now it's your turn"—he smiled—"and all you give me is words."

"I didn't say we'd do it for nothing. We do it for nothing, we're robbing the brothers!"

"You'll get some good profit out of the guns. You say they want guns down south more than they want money, so raise your price."

"Why doesn't this dude want coin? Does he think we're going to file a tax return?" asked Farnsworth.

"He wants the dope for the same reason you do. It's hard to trace and it's worth more than cash."

"No shit! I say we don't do it, Dick. It's a rip-off!"

Wager ordered another round and waited until the bartender had come and gone. "It's still a good profit for us. I'd be happy with it."

"Well, I ain't."

"Yeah. You know, I believed that crap about you two wanting to do something for La Raza. Big joke on me, right?"

"I really meant that, Gabe."

"Thanks. I'll tell the widows and orphans you really meant it. What about you, Baca? Did you mean it, too?"

"You know it."

"No, I don't. All I know is that I got those guns like I said I would, and now you two are handing me a pile of shit because you ain't getting rich enough fast enough."

"If you want to play Zorro, why don't you do it yourself?"

"Because I don't have enough dope. And by the time I get it, it'll be too late. This dude's got inventories and inspections to worry about. He's not going to wait forever."

Farnsworth finished his beer and belched slightly. "Hell, there's enough for everybody. Manny, let's at least talk to the mother. Like Gabe says, it's for a good cause."

"It sure is," said Wager.

Johnston closed the door of Sonnenberg's room against the noise from the rest of the O.C.D. offices. The inspector pointed toward the chairs and finished lighting his cigar. "Well?"

"They're not as eager as I'd like them to be," said Wager.

"How much persuasion did you use?"

"I just called them chicken-shit. Their *machismo* did the rest."

"Hmm. But they came up with the idea initially?"

Sonnenberg already knew that, but he was prodding at a possible soft spot in the case. "Yes, sir."

"Were they drinking or high at the time? Were they capable of sound judgment?"

"They had two or three beers when I was with them. I don't know if they had anything before. But my evaluation of their behavior and the questions they asked about the deal is that they were in full possession of their faculties."

It was the kind of witness-stand answer the inspector wanted. "They knew it was dangerous and they knew it was illegal, but they decided on their own to do it anyway?"

And, like every lawyer, ex-prosecutor Sonnenberg couldn't leave a thing said just one way. "Yes, sir."

"O.K.—let's go ahead, then. I've arranged to borrow the weapons from the Marine Reserve unit out at the Federal Center. The colonel and I went through law school together.

But he wasn't very eager about it—the weapons, I mean—and believe me, gentlemen, nothing had better go wrong with those weapons."

"Sweet Jesus, Inspector, that's federal property!"

"I've cleared the activity with the F.B.I., too, Sergeant. They know what's going on and will cooperate."

"Will the weapons be fully equipped, sir?" For additional security, many reserve units stored the firing pins and bolts separately from the weapons.

"A hundred percent. Ed, make arrangements for a civilian truck; and you and I will have to go out there and personally count and sign for each weapon. That's going to take time, so, Gabe, give us enough advance notice on the deal."

"Yes, sir."

"What kind of weapons and what kind of price, Inspector?"

Sonnenberg looked at Gabe for the answer.

"They'll want to talk about that with you, Ed. I mentioned shoulder weapons, handguns, and rocket launchers. I wanted to get the value as high as possible, so that Farnsworth couldn't trust anyone else to handle the deal."

"What kind of dope are they talking?"

"Coke, heroin, anything we can name."

Sonnenberg jotted some arithmetic on his pale green notepaper. Each sheet had "From the Desk of Inspector Sonnenberg" across the top, and Wager had often been tempted to reply, "Dear Desk." "Let's figure a wholesale value for the dope at . . . seventy-five thousand. They'd have paid thirty, at the most fifty percent of that?"

"Yes, sir. I'd say between fifty and seventy-five is a good range for us. It'll still give them some profit, but won't make us look too eager to do business."

Back to the little green pad. "Let's offer a hundred pistols, forty M-1 rifles, twenty M-16's, and two—make that three—rocket launchers."

Sergeant Johnston had been figuring on his notepaper. His

was white and said "From the Desk of Detective Sergeant Johnston." "That's a hell of a lot of money per weapon!"

"You got a monopoly, Ed," Wager said. "And the buyer don't have embarrassing questions. Especially about the rocket launchers and automatic weapons."

"If you want to bring the price down a bit, Sergeant, go ahead. The main thing is to set a deal with Farnsworth."

Back in his cubicle, Sergeant Johnston sighed. "I hope I don't fumble the goddam ball, Gabe. It's been a long time since I had to play the role."

"Just be yourself, Ed."

"What the hell does that mean?"

"You're a sergeant, be a sergeant."

"But I'm supposed to be a crooked sergeant!"

"Businessman, Ed. These people don't deal with crooks, they deal with businessmen. Just like they don't sell dope or run guns—they service the needs of society. And, Ed, these young folks aren't criminals; they're heroes of Aztlan, persecuted members of a counterculture striking a blow for the freedom of their downtrodden brothers."

"Oh. Well, maybe I can handle that."

# 9

Wager called from the office. The first meeting was arranged for the following afternoon.

"You're sure this sergeant's legitimate, Gabe?"

"It's my ass, too, if it doesn't work, Dick. You look him over and see if he doesn't look like every sergeant you've ever met."

"I never met any. But we'll talk to him and see how things sound."

"When can we get together? He wants to move quick."

"What's the rush?"

"He's nervous."

"Bad enough to fink?"

"Naw, just nervous. Hell, he'll be stealing half the goddam armory."

"Right. Let's meet in Left Hand Canyon. You know that little picnic area about three miles up Left Hand Creek?"

"Right side of the road?"

"That's the place. At two."

Sergeant Johnston said little on the drive up through Boulder and over the rolling highway that ran like a seam where the prairie met the mountains. The mouth of the canyon was marked by a restaurant, sprawling like a large ranch house and unlikely with its parking lot and sign in the emptiness of short grass and sloping foothills. Wager turned west on a bumpy tar road that followed the twists and angles of the narrowing valley.

"Why do they call this place Left Hand?"

"It was named after an Indian chief—Niwot. That means 'left hand' in Arapahoe." Or so a tourist guide had told him.

"Do you talk Indian, too?"

"Sure. All Hispanos do. It's part of our colorful heritage."

"Oh."

The walls of the canyon steepened into red cliffs, and the small pastures gave way to stands of leafless aspen and snow-dotted spruce and cedar. They crossed the small creek several times, and finally, at a wide curve, saw the tilting portable outhouses of the picnic area. They were painted pale green like the O.C.D. office walls, and Wager half wondered what paint salesman had a brother-in-law in the state purchasing office.

Johnston craned his neck. "The place is empty. Maybe they chickened out."

Gabe eased the Duster over the road's rough shoulder and down one of the several dirt tracks that twisted toward vandalized concrete tables and benches. The tires crackled over splintered beer bottles and past garbage-strewn ashes of old fires half hidden by windblown snow. "Let's give them time."

At ten after the hour, Baca's van, flying its red-and-black flag, coasted down the canyon and swerved toward them. It halted about twenty feet away. No one got out.

"What are they waiting for?"

"Us—we're supposed to come to them."

"Jesus. Well, let's get the crap over with."

Wager led him to the van. Baca nodded and seemed to sit the way he walked: wagging slightly from side to side with the inflated self-importance that grated on Wager. Farnsworth was not in the vehicle.

"El Taco here tells me you got something to sell."

Ed studied Baca in turn. "If the price is right."

"How much stuff you got and how much you asking?"

Ed told him.

Baca spat out the window near Wager's feet and shook his head. "We'll take ten M–16's. If we like them, we'll come back for the rest."

Wager hoped that Johnston would say the right thing. The bastard better say the right thing.

"It's a one-shot deal. All or nothing."

"You're asking for a lot of bread, Red."

"It's a lot of risk and I'm only taking it once. This is my retirement fund."

Baca started the van, and it wasn't until he spoke that Wager slowly let out his breath. "I got to talk that over; we'll see you tonight, Gabe."

They let the shiny blue van slide out of sight up the canyon before turning back toward Denver.

"How'd I do?"

"Real good, Ed. You said the right thing."

"You don't think I scared him off?"

"You said the right thing."

"You're really sure? The inspector would flip if I pushed Baca out of bounds."

"Ed, it's Baca's ball on his own ten-yard line, third and fifteen, last of the fourth, and he's down by six. If he wants to score, he's got to pass and you know it. It's your game plan, Ed."

The sergeant looked at him with surprise. "I didn't know you liked football!"

"I think it's a lousy game."

"I don't like what's going down—it's too much too fast."

"I can relate to that, Manny, I really can. But the sergeant's got a point—it's a one-shot deal." Farnsworth poured another cup of coffee from the dented aluminum pot that sat warming on top of the cabin stove. "What'd he say to you on the way back, Gabe?"

"There wasn't much to say. He wants to deal, and I think he'll come down a little. But he's only going to try it once. That's government property he'll be copping; and when it gets ripped off, this whole goddam state's going to be crawling with feds."

"I wonder how he's going to do it?"

"He says he's got a plan. Maybe he's not as dumb as he looks."

"Do you really want this?" Ramona broke her silence.

"Sure! Don't you? It's a chance to do something really important for the people," said Farnsworth.

"We can really get in over our heads, too. Manny's right for being worried. A lot can go wrong."

Gabe nodded. "That's true, Ramona. If you think it's too big, we shouldn't get in it. Maybe we shouldn't try to swim in water that's too deep."

"Are you a chicken taco now, Villanueva?" said Baca.

"I'm just saying that maybe you'd better listen to Ramona. She may be right. For a lot of people, this deal is too big."

"It ain't for me and Dick; we can handle any deal. What I don't like is the idea of maybe getting ripped off by this *cabrón* that we don't even know nothing about. We'll have a shit-pot load of dope, and all we know about this sergeant is what you told us."

"If that ain't good enough, Manny, you know where to shove it."

"Come on, you two! Cut out the *macho* crap and let's get serious. We got business to talk. Do we want this or not?"

133

"Ramona's making your decisions. Ask her."

"She's not making my decisions," said Farnsworth. "I am."

"Piss on it," said Baca. "But if something goes wrong, baby, I'll know who to blame." He gave Wager the hard eye.

"O.K., Gabe, good work!" When Sonnenberg was most excited, his voice drawled and his eyes gathered light just like the pale gray cigar smoke swirling past the window. "When do we move?"

"Let's not rush it—they're as nervous as whores in church. I said I'd talk with the sergeant and call back this morning."

The inspector raised his eyebrows at Johnston, who shrugged. "This weekend, sir?"

"Better make it a weekday. If you're with a Reserve unit, the weapons will be used on weekends," said Wager.

"Right. Let's say Monday night. That will give me and Ed time to inventory all those weapons."

"Yes, sir. Can I use your phone? Mine's an extension."

He handed Wager the red telephone. "This one's secure."

There were two places on earth where a cop felt safe enough to relax; one was at home, the other was in his unit headquarters. Now there was only one, thanks to Rietman. Wager dialed Farnsworth's number. Sonnenberg and Johnston listened. Peter answered and said "Hello" over and over until Ramona took the receiver. "This is Gabe. Tell Dick it's on for Monday night. I'll be at the Timber Line this Sunday around eight."

"Yes."

That was all. Gabe handed the telephone back to the inspector. Sergeant Johnston sighed and clapped his palms to his knees and stood. "There's the kickoff."

Twilight now came around four-thirty, but the south walls of the valleys were never in sun this late in the year, and even in the dark Wager could see the old snow pooled under the pines and cedars at the left of the highway. He slowed when the Duster tilted over the head of Boulder Canyon at Barker Reservoir. Behind the concrete dam and its row of steely fluorescent lamps, a wrinkled expanse of wind-drifted ice had settled in to wait for spring thaw. At the far end of the gray-and-white flatness huddled the twinkling cluster of soft lights that was Nederland. The voice on the car radio compared the spirit of the coming bicentennial celebration with the spirit of Christmas, and then reminded its listeners that there were only thirty shopping days left. Natividad? Little Pedro had already been talking about Santa Claus, and old Uncle Gabe was really going to bring him a surprise. Merry Christmas, kid, your old man's in the clink. Well, screw it; it wasn't his fault that Pedrocito's old man was a pusher. It was Farnsworth's own choice, and Wager was damned if he felt like taking any of the blame that belonged on Farnsworth's head. It had been his and Ramona's choice and they knew the risks. It was just too bad that the kid shared the risk but had none of the choice. Sins of the fathers. And the mothers—the women had equal rights. So many kids learned how risky life was before they learned that they had any choice; and so many never discovered that they had a choice. But Farnsworth and his wife had chosen. And they had chosen for little Peter, too.

He snapped off the radio and coasted into the twenty-five-mile-an-hour zone near the road junction that was the center of town. Most of the half-dozen stores were closed for the winter, and even the single gas station had shut down on Sunday night. The hamburger stand offered the only light against the shut wooden sides of the boxy stores and sagging garages that showed their backs across empty half-lots ridged with old snow. Wager turned down the narrow side street and crunched through the ice beside a high curb in front of the Timber Line. Baca's van sat in the crowded parking lot beside the low, log-sided building; inside, the tables were crowded with clusters of weekend skiers, red-faced and loud. Farnsworth and Baca held a table near the crackling fireplace.

135

"What's the word, man?"

"It's all set for tomorrow."

"Did you get the fucker to cut his price?"

"He says he'll come down only if the stuff is coke or heroin. He don't want nothing else."

"That's no sweat. What's his price?"

"A kilo and a half of Mexican horse, or two of coke. Top grade."

"That son of a bitch didn't come down much, did he?"

"It's his watery blue eyes. People with watery blue eyes are always greedy."

Baca grunted. "The bastard better not get greedy enough to try and rip us off."

Farnsworth leaned closer to the table, away from the noisy skiers. "We'd better set this up right; we don't want anything going wrong on this one. We'll need a truck and we'll need security."

"What's wrong with my van?" Baca asked.

"Too much weight, Manny. I can get Bruce or Jo-Jo to rent us a truck and leave it off at my place tomorrow morning. Gabe, let's meet the sergeant near Golden. I know a place just east of the Coors plant where it'll be safe to exchange."

"You'll have to show me."

"Tomorrow afternoon we'll go down and eyeball the place. It's got a fence around it—real private—but inside it's wide open so that sergeant can't pull any crap."

"He'll want to test the dope."

"He can do that while we look at the merchandise. Manny'll stay with the dope until the merchandise is transferred."

Baca tapped Wager's arm. "Alone. You tell him he comes alone."

"I'll tell him."

"Where we gonna hide all that crap, Dick?"

"I got the whole ranch; we'll just park the truck until Gabe lines up that pilot friend of his."

"If that fucking sergeant tries anything, I'm gonna waste him."

Wager asked, as mildly as he could, "You carrying a piece now?"

"I do on a deal this big," said Baca. "You don't like it?"

"If you think you need one, then I guess you'd better have it."

"If it comes time to need one, I sure as hell want it. And I'll use it."

Farnsworth hissed them quiet and stood to wave at Bruce the Juice, who stood in the doorway slowly peering around the room.

"Hey, hey—it's the frito banditos." Bruce's words slid into each other. He looked dirtier than Wager remembered, hair sprouting in different directions like a sick cat, a cushion of slow reaction between him and the world.

"Man, are you on something?"

"Oh . . ." He sank into a chair and smiled at Baca awhile before answering. "Me?"

"Dick, this turd's not going to do us no good."

"What are you dropping, Juice?"

The smile turned to Farnsworth. "Just being cool."

"No good at all," said Baca again. "Let's get Flint to do it."

Farnsworth drained his glass and studied Bruce. "You on downers now, Juice?"

"Cool, cool, cool."

Farnsworth shook his head. "Flint says he's out of the action. Him and his old lady's getting ready to move down to Taos and open up that gallery."

"He don't have to do nothing but rent the truck and turn it in when we're through. Hell, we're buddies, ain't we? Let's go talk to him."

They looked at Bruce again. "I guess we better. You coming, Gabe?"

"I want to finish my beer. I'll see you tomorrow."

"Hey—" Bruce waved at the space left by Farnsworth and Baca, and then turned slowly after them. "Hey, come here. Something to tell you."

Manny came back a step or two. "Like what?"

Bruce's arm wagged him closer. "Come here, man! Like, it's important." He grinned and waited until Baca and Farnsworth were seated again. The curious faces at the next table finally turned away.

"Well?"

"Well, the word I get's there's a fucking narc in town."

Wager sipped at his beer. In the darkness beneath the table, his heel began jiggling nervously.

"Where'd you get this word?" asked Baca.

"Where? Down in Denver. I got some connections that say we got a narc up here." Bruce grinned at each in turn. "And they're setting up a raid soon. Ain't that a rush?"

"When? What else did you hear?"

"Cool it, Gabe! Cool—no need to get your balls in an uproar."

Farnsworth glanced around the tavern's crowded tables, dwelling on a face here and there. "What did you hear about the raid?"

"I just heard there was going to be some action soon."

"When?"

"Man, I don't know. Like, narcs don't talk to me." He giggled. "And I don't want them to."

"Jesus, Dick. What do you think? Should we put the deal off?"

"You can't put it off, Dick. I already told the sergeant when, and he's got things set. He ain't gonna try it twice."

"But if it's a bad time . . ."

"When wouldn't it be a bad time!" Wager muted his anger. "It's just that we do it now or not at all. That's the choice we've got."

"Jesus, Dick."

"Look." Wager tapped the table gently. "Let's go ahead like we planned. If something pops between now and then, we can still call it off. If not, we go ahead."

Farnsworth, staring at the tabletop, nodded. "Yeah. No sense blowing our cool over shit like him." He jabbed a thumb at the smiling Bruce. "What do you think, Manny?"

"Well. Jesus."

"It's now or never, Manolito. Shit or get off the pot."

His glasses flashed as his head jerked to stare at Wager. "Let's go see Flint!"

Wager let them get through the door before leaning toward Bruce. "Where did you get your word?"

"Jeez, you're uptight, Gabe. Here." His grimy fingers probed deep into the vest pocket of his filthy army jacket and came out with a red capsule. He blew off a plume of lint and held it out. "Have a red, man—hee-hee, a redman! It'll smooth things out."

"Who have you been talking to, Bruce?"

"Just around. I mean I got contacts, too. Maybe I ain't as big as you are now, Mr. Taco-Sacko, but I can still swing some deals. Me and Jo-Jo, we do all right. And we're gonna do better! I can get some stuff that even old Farns can't come up with."

"Like what?"

"It's the greatest. Ever hear of MDA?"

"I've heard. Where are you getting it?"

"No, man, no way. You screwed old Bruce once, but not again. This is my bag, and if you want it, you got to come through me. But I'll give my old buddy a special price. I can undersell anybody in M, yeah, D, wow, A!"

"Let's go outside, Bruce."

"Naw, it's nice here. Noisy but nice. That's a nice fire. You don't want this?" He held up the capsule, then popped it in his mouth and washed it down with Wager's beer.

"Outside, Bruce, or I'll break your fucking fingers."

"Oww! Hey, man, that's not cool!" The sunburned faces at

the neighboring table swung toward them again. Wager let go of his fingers. "Man, you're coming on like a fucking narc. Maybe you're the fucking narc."

"Bruce—listen good, you cross-eyed son of a bitch."

"I'm listening."

"You say that one more time and I'll waste you."

"Hey, man, I was only joking."

"You don't joke about shit like that."

"Sure, Gabe! It was just a joke. You mad? Don't be mad; it ain't cool."

"If I hear you call me a narc again, you're dead."

"Sure, Gabe!"

"Here." He pushed the beer over to Bruce and signaled for another pitcher. "Drink up—it's all yours. But no more jokes."

"Right. No more jokes. But Jesus, you really hurt my fingers."

It was usually a forty-minute run down the canyon. Wager made it in twenty-five, halting the hot car beside a phone booth on the west edge of Boulder where a half-dozen motels tried to hide beneath low trees. Sergeant Johnston's wife answered and said, "Just a minute." In the brief wait, he heard the television quack something fatuous about the pro score roundup.

"Detective Sergeant Johnston here."

"Ed, I want a suspect picked up as soon as possible, by plainclothes officers who have no ties with any narc units." He gave the sergeant a description of Bruce the Juice.

"What's the charge?"

"Hell, I don't know—jaywalking, polluting the landscape, loud and smelly breathing. Just get him off the streets fast."

"We got to have a charge, Gabe."

"Well goddamn it think of one—you're a sergeant! Arrest the bastard on suspicion of being a bastard."

"Say, is something wrong?"

"Bruce the Juice just told Farnsworth that there's a narc up in Nederland and that a raid's planned soon. Is somebody else working up there? Is there another goddam agent fucking around up there?"

"Not that I know of. There's not supposed to be, but it could happen. Where did this Bruce get his information?"

"I don't know. He's too stoned to come across. And I can't goddamned well look too interested, can I?" He'd already risked too much with Bruce. Best just to bury him until after tomorrow.

"Right, Gabe, right—we'll get him on suspicion of burglary. Hell, we can hold him seventy-two hours on a felony charge. Say, it's still on for tomorrow, isn't it?"

"So far. Unless Bruce scares them away. We'll find out in the morning. Can you bust him real quiet? He's got to disappear without making any more waves."

"I'll get right on it."

"One more thing, Ed—if there's no other agency involved up there, where do you think Bruce got his information?"

The television music in the background rose to a familiar theme, brass and drums thumping out a call to football. "We had to inform the Nederland and Boulder authorities. Maybe one of them leaked."

"Maybe so. Maybe not."

"How many people know you're up there?"

"One too goddam many." He hung up.

Since it was Sunday, Rietman, with his seniority, did not work weekends. Wager had to wait until the next morning to talk with him.

"It'll only take a minute, Rietman."

"All right." He radioed his dispatcher the code for officer busy and not on radio. "What's so important now?"

The street was filled with bundled Christmas shoppers and the insistent clangor of a Salvation Army bell. "Let's go around the corner." He led the officer to an unused doorway drifted with blown trash. "Somebody put out the word that there's a narc up in Nederland."

"So?"

"We got somebody up there. That somebody could get blown away because of the leak. You're one of the few people who knew we were going after Farnsworth again."

"Just a fucking minute, Wager. I didn't blow nobody's cover!"

Wager looked into the angry eyes. "If I find out it was you, the word goes out about it. I won't waste time with no S.I.B. shit."

No investigation, no hearing, no fair trial, no plea—just Wager quietly telling Rietman's fellow officers that the patrolman had tipped a criminal about an agent's cover.

"Wager—Gabe—I swear to God I didn't do it!"

"We'll find out."

"It was somebody else!"

Back in his car, Wager watched Rietman's blue-and-white cruiser head slowly through the Christmas traffic toward Colfax. Maybe Rietman did it, maybe he didn't. If so, this should scare him into silence at least until after tonight. If not, Wager could apologize later. Right now, it was Gabe's own ass, and he worried about that first.

There was one more possibility and he wanted to take care of it. At the O.C.D. office, Hansen's name was logged in under "On Pager." He told Suzy to page him. Hansen telephoned in five minutes.

"Rog? This is Gabe. Somebody spilled information about our man up in the hills. If it was that whoreson Larry, he'd better learn to keep his mouth closed or I'm coming down on him. Can you get that word to him?"

"I can tell him. I don't think it was, though. He knows how to keep quiet."

"Just tell him what I said, Rog. And tell him so he believes it; I'll find out if it was him."

"Sure, Gabe." There was a note of weariness in Hansen's voice, but that was too damned bad.

Then he called Farnsworth. Little Pedro said "Hello," and called his father.

"How do you feel about it, Dick?"

"I guess it's O.K.—we haven't heard of anything going down, but nobody seems to know where the hell Bruce got to. Manny and me've been looking all over for him. Even Jo-Jo don't know where he is."

"He's probably somewhere stoned. He can't leave that shit alone any more."

"Yeah. I sure as hell don't like dealers who get hooked; they're too easy to turn. Well, come on up—I'll take you out to the place and see what you think of it."

"See you at three."

The rest of the morning dragged like a snake with a hernia. Wager did what paperwork had collected on his desk and dumped it on Suzy to polish up. Sergeant Johnston popped in to say something about moving into the last period of play as he and Sonnenberg left for the Federal Center and the armory. Ashcroft whipped through in a flurry of affidavits to give Wager a "long time no see"; Hansen did not come back to the office. At around eleven, Wager went for an early lunch at the Frontier, where Rosie did not recognize him until he spoke. Finally, he was back in his apartment trying to read a paperback history of the British commandos in World War II. The picture on the cover was more exciting than the story, which was filled with places, dates, the names of battles and roads, and the names of captains and majors and colonels. He wondered if British enlisted men ever did anything but also serve gallantly.

Giving up, he strode from one side of the room to the

other, at last stopping to survey the empty plaster wall behind the two canvas chairs. It did need something to give it
life; Billy had been right. And Wager had just the thing.
Though it wasn't that pretty picture of the Maroon Belles,
maybe it was as good. Rummaging through his closet, he
found it and wiped off the dust with a soft rag, weighing
its balance, whipping it through a series of maneuvers,
which his arm surprised him by remembering: his N.C.O.'s
sword. It's black-and-gold handle was chipped here and
there and missing an occasional screw, but the straight, dag-
gerlike blade still held its chrome finish, and the scabbard's
scratches only made it look more efficient. Etched down
the blade were the interlaced letters "United States Ma-
rines," and in a blank spot near the hilt "G. V. Wager."
He'd always wanted to hang it somewhere, though Lorraine
said she couldn't find the right spot. Now, by God, right
smack in the middle of that long, empty wall. Not that he
cared much about the Marine Corps any more, but he did
like swords and pistols. He took his time, measuring, taping,
first here, then there, finally driving the small nails and
bending them up to clamp the blade and scabbard. Billy
would like to see that.

He had also told Billy he was going to Nederland.

Shit, no! You didn't even think something like that! Billy
was his friend; Billy was his ex-partner!

He stepped back and concentrated on the sword, trying to
drive the ugly thought away.

But Billington was someone else who knew, and Wager was
a cop, and he couldn't help thinking like one. Billy just
wouldn't do it. That was all.

The wall still looked a little empty, the sword a little dwarfed
by the expanse of vacant plaster. Not Billy. It was wrong even
to think that, and Wager knew it absolutely. And Wager hated
the son of a bitch who had done it, not because it threatened

to ruin the Farnsworth case or because it might mean Wager's life, but because it made him think things like that about someone like Billy. His ex-partner had covered his back too many times; he knew Billy wouldn't do it.

"Holy Christ and the Blessed Stigmata—all those goddam guns! My back is killing me."

"I didn't know you were a Catholic," said Wager.

"I'm not," said Sergeant Johnston. "My father was. How'd you know?"

"I'm still a detective."

"Oh." Johnston geared down the sluggish truck for a series of jolting railroad tracks, then slowly picked up speed again. "You know, you're a funny guy, Gabe. Kind of like a split end way out there by yourself. I mean you're part of the team— don't get me wrong—but you take Ashcroft or Hansen, they're all lined up over the ball. You're out there by yourself."

If Wager wanted to go to confession, he'd find a priest. "Are the surveillance teams still there?"

"What? Oh." Johnston craned around to study the rear-view

mirrors. "Yeah. God, I hope nothing goes wrong. We'll all end up in Leavenworth."

"We'd have good company—governors, Cabinet members, judges."

"But we'd be locked up a hell of a lot longer than them."

True enough; he and Ed weren't governors, Cabinet members, judges. Wager glanced again at his watch; they had an hour to get through the tail end of the quitting-time traffic that still clogged Kipling Street with lines of brake lights flashing in the murky winter evening. He had met Farnsworth in midafternoon, handing him the small Christmas package. "For Pedrocito. He can open it early if he wants to."

"Hey, Gabe, that's real nice. The little guy's really hyped about Christmas this year."

"You'd better enjoy it. Kids don't stay that way very long."

"I know." He casually tossed the red-and-green package onto the cowhide couch. "The sergeant's all set? I'm getting high about this deal. You know, this is really big-time shit if we pull it off."

"He's loading the truck now, I guess."

"Great. Let's go look at the meet. See if you think it's all right."

It was an hour's ride down through Boulder and along the Foothills Highway, with its inevitable stretches of wind-drifted snow mashed into sheet ice. At Golden, Farnsworth turned east on Forty-fourth Avenue past the concrete blocks of the Coors factory and the string of box and tank cars that always stood waiting. "It's just up here—this storage lot." A narrow dirt road led to a side entry in a high slat fence. The compound inside was littered with rusting pipe, large cable spools, stacks of snowy two-by-fours warping slowly.

"What about security patrols?"

"It's a private system; the watchman's a friend of mine. That's how I know about this place. He won't check it until after midnight."

"What about our own security?"

"We meet the sergeant in the middle where it's open. You tell him to park right there. Baca'll be sitting over there in our truck. You and me, we check out the merchandise; if it's O.K., Baca brings out the dope."

"And if it's not?"

Farnsworth stared at Wager. "You said you grooved on this dude, Gabe."

"I do. But we're talking just in case."

"O.K. Just in case he's selling us a wolf ticket, Baca's carrying iron. If that son of a bitch tries anything, he's had the cock."

"I think he's straight."

"Just make sure he comes alone."

He and Johnston were alone in the truck, anyway. The two cars with the inspector and the surveillance teams trailed a hundred yards back as they turned west on I-70 and Wager pressed his transmit key. "Two-one, this is two-one-two."

"Go ahead." The inspector's voice was slightly muffled; he was probably lighting another maduro.

"We're about a half-mile from the place. Ten seventy-seven in twenty minutes."

"Ten-four. Make your turn; we'll double back."

"Ten-four."

Johnston steered the spongy truck down the long curve of freeway. "You think they'll try to rip me off?"

The thought had entered Wager's head. "What choice do we have?"

Johnston pondered. "Yeah."

"They didn't talk rip-off to me. Just go through with it like we planned."

"O.K. The way we planned."

The truck edged into the line of cars creeping off the freeway at the Ward Road interchange.

"They really need a traffic light here."

"File a complaint with the traffic division."

"Hell of a lot of good it would do." Ed finally saw an opening to swing the truck toward West Forty-fourth Avenue and out beyond Mount Olivet Cemetery. They rode without speaking; the heavy truck squeaked with the ripples of the two-lane asphalt.

Wager squinted into the darkness against the glare of oncoming traffic. "Slow down; we're getting close." Past the advertisement for the railroad museum, he saw the landmark. "There—we turn at that white sign."

"The white sign."

Wager keyed the radio: "Here we go."

"Ten-four" came Sonnenberg's lazy voice.

"Here we go," echoed Ed, and swerved the wheel. Wager saw the two unmarked cars flash by as the string of urgent traffic pent up by the truck sped past.

"We're a little early."

"They won't mind," said Wager.

The rocking headlights picked out the fence, with its boards bending out here and there away from the wire mesh.

"There's the gate. Hold up, I'll open it."

Gabe hopped out into the icy wind that funneled down between North and South Table Mountains, bringing little ice crystals that melted like mist on his face. He fumbled at the metal latch with stinging fingers; then, with a creak, the heavy gates swung in. He held one back while the truck ground by, then quickly climbed back into the cab.

"Jesus, it's cold! Pull the truck right over there—that open area."

"Did you see anybody?" Johnston set the brake and turned off the lights, leaving the motor running for heat.

"No."

Silence. The wind thumped against the truck's sides and jiggled it slightly.

"I'll bet those guys on surveillance are freezing their balls off."

They should be moving along the outside of the fence by now. And they would be cold. "Yes."

"Something bugging you? You think something's wrong?"

Billy wouldn't do it. "No."

"They're late."

He knew Billy wouldn't do it. "Yes."

More silence; more wind. His eyes slowly grew accustomed to the darkness and he could see the wisps of dry snow smoke across the ground in the wind. Best not to think of Billy. Right now, everything was right here. It was Farnsworth only. Right now.

"Is that them?" Slits of light moved through the boards as headlights glided down the fence. Wager didn't bother to answer; they would know soon enough.

The creak of the gate was barely audible over the wind; the headlights swung in, paused, the gate clanged shut, then the rented truck moved past Wager's side, Farnsworth's face pale in the dash light's reflection. Wager clicked his transmit button three times, then hid the radio pack inside his parka.

"Where's he going?"

"Over by the spools. Baca will cover the deal from there."

"Oh. Yeah. You said." Johnston cracked his knuckles. "Blessed baby Jesus, I hope everything goes O.K."

"Kill the engine; let's go say hello."

Farnsworth met them halfway between the trucks. He held a flashlight in one hand and shined it briefly on Johnston and Wager. "Everything all right?"

"Fine. Come on, it's fucking cold."

They turned to Johnston's truck and clambered into the back; their breath frosted in the flashlight's beam, but at least the truck walls blocked the wind.

"Goddam—they're all in boxes!"

"What'd you expect?" asked Johnston. "They always come that way. They're packed for transport."

"Let's see them. I want to see what I'm getting for all that dope."

Johnston began twisting the butterfly nuts off the lid of an olive-drab box. "Where's the stuff?"

"It's in my truck. Let me see these babies; then we'll go over." Farnsworth raised the lid and shined the light over six M-1 rifles nested butt to muzzle in the narrow pine box. "Beautiful. Dy-no-mite! Where's the rocket launchers?"

"Over here." Johnston pointed at the folded tubes of painted alloy. "They twist together like this."

"Beautiful. The M-16's? The pistols?"

"In here." He tapped two stacks of shorter, fatter boxes and shifted with cold as Farnsworth opened one and peered in.

"Come on, Dick, it's getting cold."

"Man! It makes me feel ten feet tall just to look at this stuff! I got to have one of these for myself!"

Gabe jabbed an elbow into the silent sergeant's ribs. "Oh," he said. "I want to see the dope. Then we move the guns."

"It's there, man, it's there."

"Let's see it, then."

Farnsworth clicked off the flashlight and jumped down to the frozen earth. Wager and Johnston followed him through the wind to the lee side of the orange rental truck. Farnsworth gave a thumbs-up sign; Baca unlocked the cab door and Johnston climbed in beside him. Wager and Farnsworth stamped their feet and waited beside the front fender.

"He's all alone?"

"Like you said." Wager blew on his hands and jammed them back into his pockets. "Why?"

"Because we're taking him. When he comes out of the cab with his hands full of dope, you and me grab him and Manny comes down on him from behind."

Wager's surprise was genuine. "You said it was a straight deal!"

"Baca and me changed our mind. This dude's cutting into our profit margin, and we don't owe him a thing."

"Listen, that son of a bitch'll come after us—I know these army bastards, and he'll take it personal." A rip-off meant greater risk; it meant that the targets became the hunters; it meant guns and more danger at an already chancy moment.

"He'll be too busy skipping from the feds to worry about us —me and Baca already talked it over. We got him by the balls. It's all his risk, and he won't be able to do a thing about it."

"If we pull this shit, he's gonna turn state's evidence just to get even. And he knows a lot about me."

"Yeah. I didn't think of that." Farnsworth rubbed a mitten under his nose. "Son of a bitch."

"Let's play him straight. We got to."

"He might fink on us anyway. Even if we play him straight, he might fink if something happens."

"With the dope, he's got a reason not to. Was this your idea or Baca's?"

"Manny's. But it sounded pretty good."

Wager could see Baca's plan: the big rip-off and the only one left to feel the heat would be Gabe Villanueva. "Did Baca tell you to tell me that you would keep my cut for me?"

"Yeah! He said you'd have to dig a hole somewhere and we'd finish the deal and we'd hold your split until you came up again."

Sure they would. Good old Manny—a real Aztec prince. "He told you wrong. He's setting me up. You better play that sergeant straight, because I'm going to be all over you like stink on shit if you don't. If you make me a pigeon, I'm making you hot. Play him honest, Dick!"

Doubt, fear, desperation—even in the dim light of the snow, Wager saw all those things in Farnsworth's face. "It's too fucking late—Manny thinks it's all set up."

As he spoke, the handle of the orange door bobbed and it swung open to show Ed's shadow bent to step down from the cab. "It tests O.K."

Wager cursed and grabbed Farnsworth's parka and threw the surprised man aside. "Ed—drop!"

Wordless, Johnston plunged for the ground; over his shoulder, Baca raised high in the seat, his dim arm groping inside his coat. Wager tugged at the familiar .45 shoved in the back of his pants and cursed again as the sight blade snagged on his underwear. He yanked savagely at the handle, freeing it with a ripping sound.

Baca beat him. In one of those moments when everything slowed and his eyes saw everywhere, Wager watched Baca's arm pull from beneath the red down vest, a stubby-barreled small-caliber revolver in his hand. On the ground, Farnsworth and Johnston stared at Wager, one frozen in the act of pushing up with both hands, eyes still wide and jaw sagging; the other as surprised but already, with a cop's reflexes, bending his arm behind his back for the pistol stuffed there. Baca's revolver swung toward him and in the glow of the dash lights, Wager saw the greasy glint of bullets in the drum's chambers. And, beneath it all and somewhere in the back of his mind, he thought how cold it was.

His own pistol was half raised when Baca fired.

The orange flash blinded him, and stinging heat whipped across his face. Wager felt his own weapon buck against his hand as the shot went wild and he flung himself aside, grinding the glare out of his eyes with his fingers, twisting under the truck for cover.

"Police! Don't move!" Ed's voice howled from somewhere near the right front tire, and now Wager could see Farnsworth on hands and knees scuttling for the large wooden spools. The truck's motor suddenly roared and the vehicle lurched forward, Gabe squirming to pull his legs from under the wheels. He yanked out the radio pack and aimed the antenna at the fence.

153

"We're blown. Baca's in the truck. Armed. He's going for the gate!"

"Ten-four." The inspector sounded almost bored.

The truck's differential swung just over his head and Wager darted for Farnsworth as the tailgate cleared him. "Down, you fucker—down and spread!"

"What is this? What the shit is this?"

"It's a bust!"

Johnston kicked Farnsworth's legs apart and slapped at his body; Wager twisted the man's arms behind him and clamped the irons around his wrists. "Ed—you got the keys! Get the truck behind Baca—block him off!"

"What? Oh—yeah!" He stumbled toward the vehicle; even in haste, his long body curved at the shoulders like a question mark.

"You're a fucking cop? You?"

"You got a right to remain silent, you son of a bitch, and you better use it." Wager watched Baca's truck rumble in screaming low gear for the closed gate. Ed clambered into his cab and turned on the headlights. Jesus, thought Wager, it's a wonder he didn't stop to check the oil. Then the lights dimmed and brightened as the vehicle started and rolled forward.

Baca hit the gate with the splintering sound of bolts pulled through wood, wheeled left to snag the gatepost with the truck body, and yanked to a halt in a swirl of powdery snow as headlights bounded down the fence toward him. Ed thumped the rear of Baca's truck with his bumper, and in the glare of headlights spotlighting the cab, Wager saw Baca's door open cautiously, two empty hands spread high and tensely still over the window frame. At Wager's feet, the silent Farnsworth, face almost as pale as the patches of snow, stared up at him.

Baca and Farnsworth were already in separate holding pens at Main Headquarters by the time Wager, driving the rental truck, arrived. Johnston and the inspector were still unloading and re-inventorying the weapons for an anxious marine colonel. Wager filled out an impound order on the truck and checked in the keys; Flint would have some explaining to do to the rental agency, and wasn't that too goddam bad. Tucking under his arm the two square bundles wrapped in newspaper and masking tape, Wager headed for the custodian's office.

"Hey—Gabe! Detective Wager!" Through the bustling uniforms and confusion of the retiring shift, Gargan, the police reporter, wagged a hand at Wager. "Wait a minute!"

There were a lot of things Wager didn't need right now. One of them was Gargan.

"Hey, I hear you pulled off a heavy bust!" Beneath the worn sheepskin coat peeked Gargan's inevitable black turtleneck. "How about something on it, Gabe? Is that the dope there?"

With the caution he could never quite hide around newsmen, Wager nodded. "We got a couple kilos of coke."

"What's it worth?"

"Street value, maybe five or eight hundred thousand. But listen, there's no story in it yet."

"No story? That's got to be the biggest bust in the state! Come on, man, what happened?"

"I can't open it up yet, Gargan. There's still a lot of loose ends. As soon as things are ready, I'll give you a call."

"Yeah? That's what you said about that Alvarez bust, too; and a hell of a lot of good you did me."

Wager had forgotten that one. Somehow, there always seemed to be something more important to do than talk to reporters. "I'm sorry about that. This time for sure."

"If I don't get it from you, I'll get it from somebody else. It may not be as good, but by God I'll get a story!"

"Then talk to Sonnenberg. He should be in soon." That's what inspectors were paid for; they always thought reporters were important.

"Where is he? Who else was in on it?"

"He's on pager." Wager pulled away and headed down the

tan hallway toward the property room. "Tell the shift sergeant you're trying to reach him."

"Can I use your name? Thanks, Gabe!"

Officer Green was on duty in the custodian wing; she whistled slightly when Wager set the bundles on the counter. "Is that all for real?"

"That's what the lab's supposed to tell me."

"Gosh—I've never seen so much." She initialed the large evidence bag and slipped the packages inside and then wound the tape tightly.

Wager filled out a laboratory analysis request while she placed the bag in the safe. "Have the lab give me a call as soon as the test is run."

"Yes, sir."

The next stop was the booking desk. A sergeant who looked as if his retirement date was circled on his calendar glanced at Wager and then turned back to his newspaper.

"I'm Detective Wager, Sergeant. Can you tell me if either Farnsworth or Baca have posted bond yet?"

"Wager?" He peered at Gabe's face. "I didn't recognize you with all the face hair."

"I'm on assignment."

"Right, right—everybody grows a beard on assignment. Let's see," he slowly drew his thumb down a ledger. "Farnsworth and Baca, Baca and Farnsworth. Yep, here they are. And nope, no bond yet. They're still up in the pens. Felony bonds are posted only during working hours in front of a judge. You want to see them?"

"I've seen enough of them."

"Seen one, seen them all."

"Can you tell me if a flake was brought in late yesterday, maybe early this morning?"

"Name?"

"Hornbacher, Bruce."

Again the slow thumb whispering down the page of the

ledger. "Detective Austin was the minion who harassed that poor innocent lad."

"Can I talk with him?"

"I don't believe you're the officer of record, Detective Wager. Ain't you read the latest law bulletin?" This week's area of legal uncertainty concerned the authority to interview prisoners; some judge in a federal court somewhere had bought what some lawyer had argued about extended hearsay, and so far no prosecutor had come up with a rebuttal.

"Is Austin the one in Crimes Against Persons?"

"The same."

"Can I use your phone?"

"Official call?"

On this side of the law, there were few things he disliked more than a philosophical Irish cop with more hash marks than days to retirement. "Yes, Sergeant. It's an official call."

"Keep it short. Them's regulations."

The dispatcher took Wager's request, and in a few minutes Austin telephoned.

"Can you meet me at Main Headquarters? I've got to talk to one of your prisoners, Hornbacher."

"How soon?"

"The sooner the better."

In the pause, Wager heard the background commotion: a drunk howling "No! Fuck you all! No!"; a woman crying nasally with snagging breaths; an official voice saying, "Over here —bring the stretcher over here." "Man, I'm up to my eyes in shit right now. I'll try to get over there, but I sure as hell can't promise."

"Hang on a minute." He turned to the desk sergeant. "Can he give authorization by telephone?"

The sergeant rubbed the bristles of his chin. "I don't know —be worth a try. You got to state your exact purpose in interviewing said suspect."

"Austin? My exact purpose in interviewing said suspect is to determine his alleged involvement in local narcotics operations. Now tell the sergeant I can talk to the turd." He handed over the receiver.

"Yeah, Detective Austin, it's me. . . . O.K." The sergeant hung up and made a note. "He'll be in Room 2 in about twenty minutes."

"Fine."

There was one more telephone call he had to make, but this one was unofficial. And he didn't want that red-beaked Mick cop listening anyway. He spun the pay phone's dial in a familiar series, and Ramona said, "Hello."

"This is Gabe. Dick and Manny were busted."

"Oh, Jesús María!"

"Ramona—I'm a narc. I busted them."

In the long silence, he could hear the dog barking faintly outside the cabin. "You son of a bitch. You *cabrón pinche*. I guess you're happy."

"I am. I am God damned happy there's two less pushers on the street, and this is no apology."

"So you're calling to tell me how happy you are."

"I'm calling to say that Dick will be doing your time, too. But if there's something you and Pedro need—if you need help getting to see Dick—let me know and I'll do what I can."

"I don't need your help. We don't want your help."

"They're in Main Headquarters, down in Denver."

She hung up before he did.

Wager used the rest of the time and the silent interrogation room to fill out the form for ammunition expended in the line of duty. Thank God he hadn't hit Baca: the paperwork on a wounded or slain suspect was endless. He closed his eyes to picture the truck's cab and where he had stood in relation to Baca, where he had fired, where the bullet seemed to have gone: Baca's arm lifting the small pistol from under his down vest, swinging the muzzle toward him, and the tenseness and acid burning and even sweat that came stronger now with his

158

eyes closed than when he had slid aside through slowly yielding air to force his own pistol up against the weight of an endless moment, Baca's weapon spurting heat and stinging flecks of burning powder across his face and eyeballs, and Wager, even as he fired, waiting for the punch of the round, the numbness, the expected surprise of being hit. He opened his eyes and drew in a long, slow breath; the dim wall of the interrogation room hung blankly just beyond the light over the interview table. From the plastic compound of its top came that familiar odor of rancid sweat, sour sponge water, old cigarette smoke. Baca had missed; so had Wager. He noted the probable direction of his round—somewhere into the floorboard on the rider's side of the cab. He wrote "unobserved" for Baca's round; it was enough that Baca had missed.

"You Detective Wager?"

A uniformed policeman led Bruce the Juice into the small room and looked at him dubiously.

Wager nodded. "I'll give you a call when we're through. Well, Brucie, it's good to see you here."

Hornbacher stared at Wager and then tried to spit; it came out a fluffy white bubble that rested on the stringy hair of his chin. Wager stood and smiled. "Sit down, Brucie."

"I'll stand, you fucking pig. I should of known you was a fucking pig."

Wager's fist jabbed out to clamp Bruce's thin neck, and the soft flesh and cords squeezed in his fingers like rotten fruit— like Ramona and Baca and Rietman squeezed to pulp in his hand.

"Cut it out! You're hurting me! Guard!"

The policeman's worried face swung into the open door. "Hey, hey—let's take it easy, now!"

Wager shoved the clammy flesh from him, bouncing Bruce into the dark green chair and wiping his hand to rid it of the oily, pimply, dirty slime that he had bathed himself in for the last months. "I'm going to take you away from all this, Brucie."

"Did you hear that? Did you hear what he said? He's going to waste me!"

"No, I didn't hear it. You can file a complaint if you want. Maybe I'd better stay in the room, Detective Wager."

"That's O.K., Officer. Mr. Hornbacher and me are through."

"Already? You want me to take him back now?"

"I do."

Wager stood rigid until their steps had faded into the general rustle of movement that always filled the restless building. He had been stupid, he knew; it was dumb enough to lean on a prisoner around witnesses, but dumbest of all was to lose his temper. The brief pleasure of breaking Bruce's goddamned neck could be paid for by the loss of months of work. He sucked another deep breath of stale air and rubbed his grainy eyes and stood quite still until he felt his self-control gain over the tense muscles of his back and chest and neck. It was all a game; you had to remember that. The pay was the same, and if you took the game seriously you could lose it all.

"That was quick." The Irish sergeant's eyes studied Wager.

"He didn't have much to say. He's due for release. I'd like to give him a ride home."

Again the eyes, distant, weighing. "If he's released, he won't have to go with you."

"So don't tell him, Sergeant. You're not a lawyer."

"I'm not a narcotics agent, either, Detective."

The slight Spanish lilt came: "And that means what?"

"That means you got your ways of doing things and I got mine. I'd just as soon keep them separate."

Seldom did the dislike of the other branches of police work for narcotics agents come out, but Wager knew it was always there. The others didn't have to reach so deep into shit. They didn't like the stench that came with that reach. "I want to talk with the man, Sergeant. If he does not like my questions, he can file a complaint."

160

"It's your career."

"It is. Just tell him I'm giving him a ride home."

"We'll see what Austin says first." He pressed the transmit button of the desk radio.

"I'll be in Room 2 working on affidavits."

The paperwork went slowly; he tried to list the events of the investigation and bust, but the effort was broken by his mind's turning from Bruce to Ramona to Rietman to Billy. First the possible rip-off of evidence, then a tip on a fellow officer. And God only knew how much more that had not surfaced yet.

He was halfway through the "details" section of the arresting officer's report when his radio pack sounded his number. "Ten-ninety-one at Sergeant Ahern's desk."

"Ten-four."

Pick up a prisoner at the booking sergeant's desk. Wager arrived in time to see Bruce the Juice counting the change from his personal-effects envelope.

"Hello again, Bruce."

The youth's face sagged into a gray color. "Hey, Sergeant. What's this guy doing here?"

"It's a democracy, sonny. And this is a public building."

Wager smiled. "I've been assigned to escort you home safely."

"No way—come on, Sergeant. I ain't going with him!"

"You're released, Hornbacher. We got no jurisdiction. Just sign that personal-effects form and get out."

"But . . . But . . ."

Wager's hand gripped the thin arm. "Let's go, Bruce. I'll even buy you a beer on the way."

# 11

Bruce sagged in Wager's car, head jiggling loosely against the window glass, weary eyes sliding past the streetlights, past the occasional lumpy pedestrians who walked rapidly from the snowy parking lots to the municipal auditorium, past the restless youths huddled in a cold line outside a nightclub featuring Freddie Henchie and the Soul Setters. The nervous energy Bruce had inside headquarters was gone now, and thin lines of sweat filled the creases on his forehead. Wager let him sweat.

They turned west on Sixth Avenue and crossed the series of narrow viaducts, then dipped beneath overpasses and behind the high concrete revetments that collected the rattle of traffic and brown slush dropped like manure from snow-packed fenders. Bruce finally licked his chapped lips and half turned his head. "Where we going?"

"I told you. I'm taking you home. You look like you need a rest."

Bruce had come down fast in the last twenty-four hours—his face sagging and yellow, his thin hands clusters of fingers gripping each other because there was nothing else to hold. Gradually, Gabe's words elbowed through the woolly layers to mean something. "What for?"

"I want people to see that we're good friends."

"I ain't friends with no pig!"

"You and I know that."

Another silence. Wager heard the sticky sound of Bruce's tongue peeling from the roof of his dry mouth. "I don't want nobody to think we're friends."

"Me either—but that's what I got to do."

"You just let me out. I can get home all right."

"Relax. Enjoy the ride. I'll even buy you a beer at the Timber Line when we get there. By the way, I busted Farnsworth and Baca tonight." He nudged the loose shoulder. "Did you hear me?"

"What? You what?"

"I busted Farnsworth and Baca tonight."

"No shit! What'd you get them on?"

"Conspiracy to sell, selling, possession, and assaulting an officer with a deadly weapon."

"Old Farns and Manny! I'll be Goddamned." The news worked through the padding of his drug hangover to wake him up. "Those fuckers had it coming. But Jesus, there's going to be some bopping when the system dries up." He fell silent picturing the shifting routes of supply, the sudden jumps in prices, the scramble for new sources, the possibilities that opened for him. And then something else. "Hey, Villanueva—the whole town is gonna know who busted him. And you want to take me to the Timber Line for a friendly beer?"

The soft smile was in Wager's voice as well as on his lips. "That's right."

"No way! I ain't finked and I ain't getting burned by you!"

"Now, now, they'll just think you're a good citizen showing a little civic pride by having a beer with the arresting officer."

"No—you ain't got nothing on me."

"After they see you with me, I won't need anything on you."

"They'll know I was clean. They'll believe me before they believe any goddam narc."

"Maybe. And maybe not. I always thought Jo-Jo was a little nuts. I'll bet your ass I can make him believe you turned."

"No way. Jo-Jo's my buddy. You can't shit him about me."

"You know what I'll tell him? I'll say that you knew I was a narc when you brought me in. I'll say that I told you to spread the word just before I popped Farnsworth that there was a narc in town. That way nobody would lay the bust against you. You know that son of a bitch has fried brains—he's going to believe my rap just long enough to plant some lumps on your skull, Brucie."

From the corner of his eye, Wager saw Bruce's face wince against the ache of his head and the weight of Gabe's words.

"Tell me you don't think he's a crazy bastard, Brucie."

Silence.

"Tell me you don't think he might cut you up before you can say diddly shit."

"Why?" Bruce's dry voice barely carried over the smack of tires on the wet highway. "Why this action?"

"Figure it out: I want something from you."

"Like what?"

"Like where did you get your information about a narc up in Nederland."

"That's all you want?"

"That'll do for starters."

"Listen, can we stop and get a drink somewhere? I'm hurting."

164

Wager spotted the neon cocktail glass of a roadside bar, and turned in to the parking lot. The Juice's hand was on the door handle before the car stopped. Wager grabbed the arm of Bruce's Levi jacket and pulled his pistol from the waist of his trousers. "See this?" The chrome angles of the weapon glinted in the blue neon.

Bruce sat very still. "What's that for, man?"

"It's for you if you try to cut out on me. I'll blow you in half."

Again the faintly sticky sound from Bruce's mouth before he spoke. "I wasn't even thinking of that. I just wanted to stop for a drink. If you don't really want one, man, just say so."

"Sure I do, Brucie." He patted the bony shoulder beneath the grime-slick cloth. "It's a real pleasure to spend a quiet hour with you."

He placed Bruce next to the wall in the dark leatherette booth. A girl in a frilly skirt and black mesh stockings smiled for their order. In the dim blue light, her lipstick looked black. Wager waited until the drinks were brought before speaking.

"The information—where'd you get it?"

"God, that's good! God, I was thirsty."

"Where?"

"From that guy named Larry."

"The one who set me up with you?" Wager brought him up in memory: white male, slender build, mid-thirties, straight hair slicked back into a curly fringe just over his collar.

"Yeah. That bastard. We were working on this big deal and he says, 'You better play it cool.' 'Why?' I says. 'There's a narc up there,' he says. 'He ain't after you now, but if you get too big he will be.' 'Who is it?' I says. And the fucker said he didn't know. The son of a bitch put you on me and then he said he didn't know you."

"What the hell did you expect him to say, Brucie? What the hell would you say?"

"Yeah? Well, I wouldn't pull nothing like that. He's a son of a bitch."

"When did he tell you about the raid?"

"At the same time. He said I wouldn't have to stay low for long—that the narc—you—was gonna wrap things up in a few days, and then I could start moving my stuff."

"Where'd he get his word?"

"He said he had a pipeline with the man."

"What kind of pipeline?"

"That's all he said and that's all I asked." Bruce rattled the cubes in his empty glass. "How about another?"

Wager signaled the black mesh stockings.

"It don't sound good, does it, Villanueva?" Bruce's teeth showed dimly beneath his thin mustache. "I mean it sounds like some fucking cop just might be doing a number, don't it?"

It did. It all figured up in ways Wager didn't like. He swallowed a mouthful of beer that tasted flat and sour and watery. "I'd like to know more about that pipeline."

Bruce's eyes narrowed over the rim of his glass. "I bet you would."

In the eyes, in the mockery, Wager saw the erosion already at work. One bad cop—one cop who was no better than the puke he was supposed to be wiping up—and scum like that across the table laughed to see it happen. "You want to tell me how much you like it?"

The eyes slid away. "Naw, man. I'm just agreeing with you. I bet you would like to know more about that pipeline. That's all."

"I'm glad that's all. What kind of deal did you and Larry set up?"

Bruce rattled the suddenly empty glass. Wager ordered another for him, and mesh stockings said, "My, we're a thirsty boy tonight, aren't we?" He waited until Bruce was sucking at the next glass and then repeated the question.

"I don't think I got to answer that. I think I got some rights under the Fifth Amendment, Mr. Narc."

"That booze is lifting you up again, Bruce. I can fix it so

166

you'll come down fast. I can send you places where you won't get even a sniff of pot."

He swallowed. "That don't shake me. I can get off this stuff any time I want, and it don't shake me at all."

"I want something on Larry that will lead me to that pipeline. I don't give a damn about you or your deal—unless you make it important. Then I'll shake you like a fucking rug. Now, what were you putting down?"

"You want me to set him up with you?"

"What'd he do to you?"

"Yeah. Yeah, he did that, didn't he?"

"What was your deal?"

"You won't hassle me on this? I mean I got some stuff that I want to move; it ain't for me—it's for my old lady's kid; he's got spasms or something and needs a specialist. What doctor's gonna do something for nothing?"

Wager didn't care who it was for. "I'll let you take your crap out of the state and work somewhere else."

Bruce chewed the thin fringe of hair on his lip. "I can just take all my stash and leave—that's what you mean?"

Wager said yes. And it was true. The Juice would take his fall sooner or later, either busted or hooked. Turds like him were mashed all the time.

"O.K.—it's a deal. Here's the action: Larry got ahold of some MDA, real quality stuff, and wanted to sell it cheap. He said he had to move it fast."

"Why?"

"I don't know. At the price he wanted, I wasn't asking. Anyway, me and Jo-Jo got some bread together and went in heavy, you know? This MDA is something that even Farnsworth ain't got. And it was really a good deal."

"And?"

"And that's it. Jo-Jo and me put the money down and Larry gave us five pounds of pure."

"This is when he told you about the agent in Nederland?"

"Yeah. Ain't that a bitch?"

"Was Jo-Jo with you then?"

"Naw. Him and his old lady was working another deal in Fort Collins. I ain't seen Jo-Jo since the deal with Larry went down. Shit, I was having a drink at the Timber Line—you remember, you bought me a whole pitcher of beer—and I farted around there a couple hours and then I went out to my car, and the man takes my elbow and says, 'Let's go.' We must of rode around four hours before he finally brought me in, and then nobody even let me make my goddam phone call. They just put me in a cage and forgot about me—it was unreal, man! Talk about your police state! I bet old Jo-Jo's crapping little blue pills. We put down a lot of bread and I didn't get to tell him where the stash is."

"I hope he gives you time to explain."

"He'll be all right—all he's got to do is see the stuff. He's just a little bit crazy, you know?"

"You two better have your look while you're moving that crap out of the state."

He let Bruce off in the pines at the south edge of town. "I want to walk from here, man," Bruce said. "I don't want no more to do with you."

"That makes us both happy. You haul your tail by tomorrow night."

"Right on, pig. And, say, good luck with that Larry son of a bitch. I really mean that."

It was after one when he reached the Denver city limits, and there was nothing he could do until morning. He was tired; his eyes stung from the headlights bursting in the dirt of his windshield, and he had that dull headache that comes with hunger and weariness. In his apartment, he rummaged through the refrigerator for the makings of a Marine Corps omelette, and when all the odds and ends had been chopped and tossed into the simmering pool of egg, he opened the last beer. So Larry had a pipeline. What the hell connection was there

168

between Larry and Rietman? Larry was Hansen's snitch, although that wouldn't keep him and Rietman apart. And Rietman had known that the O.C.D. was putting an agent in Nederland; Wager himself had told him. He folded the egg into a thick roll, carefully tucking the edges against spilling the vegetables and meat and cheese from the bed of yellow. Then he chewed with his mind as well as with his mouth: Rietman would not have had to tell Larry about the agent, since Larry had been the initial contact for Wager. But the time of the bust was something else; someone else had to tell Larry that they were getting close to Farnsworth. Wager had told Rietman there in the drive-in; he had wanted to see what the reaction would be—to give Rietman a chance. And what had happened? Either everything or nothing; for the life of him, Wager did not know if Rietman had been lying.

After washing the dishes and finally stretching out on his bed, Wager closed his eyes and went over the memories again; and despite the relief his body felt at lying flat and motionless, his mind would not rest. He should have known it wouldn't. Larry was the key right now, and by the Lord's crown wouldn't he like to have him for five minutes! Wager felt his body clenching and forced himself to breathe deeply, slowly, telling himself that the undercover act was over—he could relax now. Beneath his closed eyelids, he felt the graininess squeeze weary moisture from his eyes. It had not been the best bust in the world. He could still see the ragged blossom of orange fire spraying toward him, feel the whip of burning powder across his face, even hear . . . No, he hadn't heard anything then. Strange. But now it seemed he could hear the sizzle of the round past his ear. And see his own gun so slow to lift, to turn, to fire. He caught his muscles drawing up again and spread himself over the bed to let his flesh sag loosely. Maybe he should take up yoga. Maybe he should take a vacation. Maybe, like Lorraine had said, he was a little nuts. Crap. It had been a lousy bust and there was a rotten cop somewhere. And Larry was the key. Larry—the name jiggled something; Wager clicked on the lamp and padded across the rug to the little notebook in the hip pocket of his pants hanging on the doorknob. He hoped the faint memory was wrong; he hoped that the only possible link he knew between Larry and any other cop was Hansen or Rietman. But there on an almost empty page of his notebook was an entry made six months ago: Larry Ginsdale, Oscar Pitkin, and Billington's initials after them. Billy had asked Gabe if he had heard of them; two heads from California who had begun dealing in large quantities of coke. It might not even be the same Larry. There were a lot of Larrys. Even if it was, it couldn't mean anything. Billington had been his partner, and a man learned all there was about his partner. Billy just wouldn't do it.

The restless turning had finally rolled into a blackness that was more like passing out than sleep, and it took the alarm to pull him out of the dark. Coffee was enough for breakfast; however, he soaked in a hot shower and took his time to shave off his beard. The newly exposed flesh was pale and soft, and the razor kept snagging in tiny cuts. But the clean feeling was worth the shreds of toilet paper stuck here and there to little bloody dots. And the shaving took his mind off the worries that had filled it the night before. He slid behind the wheel of his familiar car and automatically clicked on the police radio. The routine queries and replies began to weave him back into the familiar fabric of police routine, and by the time he arrived at the O.C.D. parking lot, he felt better; he felt like Gabe Wager, cop.

Mrs. Gutierrez smiled as she pressed the "open" buzzer. "My, you look happy today, Detective Wager."

"I feel clean."

She was puzzled. "Clean? Oh—you shaved! Too bad; I kind of liked your beard."

"Yes, ma'am."

Sergeant Johnston was not yet in his cubicle. Wager went to his desk for the morning's first thermos of coffee and the stack of paperwork still unfinished from last night's business. Keeping an ear open for the sound of Johnston's voice, he burrowed into the arresting officer's report. Maybe it wasn't such a bad bust after all. In fact, the more he studied it in the morning light, the better it looked.

Suzy came in with the pile of morning mail. "Gabe, were you in on that big bust last night?"

"Yes."

"Everybody's saying it's the biggest the O.C.D.'s ever had. There's a reporter, Gargan, who's been calling for you since I came in."

"Tell him I'm in a meeting. Has Johnston come in yet?"

"I think he's in the inspector's office."

Wager walked the few steps down the narrow hall to Sonnenberg's door; it was closed. He went back to his desk and tried to concentrate on completing the arrest report. Finally he heard the inspector's door open.

"Ed, can I see you?"

"Come in—I want to see you, too." Johnston sat on the cushioned swivel chair behind his desk and propped his feet on one of the pulled-out drawers. "Wow—I'm still tired from last night. My back! Say, thanks again, Gabe. I really didn't know what that bastard was up to when you yelled." The balding head bobbed on the end of its tilted neck. "The inspector's really happy with most of the case."

"Most of it? I thought he'd be pretty God damned happy with all of it."

"Sure, we got them on the important stuff. But he's still worried about entrapment. He thinks the defense is going to try to blitz that one at the advisement."

"The defense always tries everything."

"Well, the inspector wants Farnsworth real bad, that's all. He sees this as our chance to bid for a statewide narcotics agency, and he's uptight about it. The advisement's set for this afternoon. How soon can we huddle with the D.A.'s office?"

"Any time. But we've got other business, too."

Johnston's watery eyes narrowed. "You have something new on that?"

He told him what Bruce the Juice had said.

"Have you talked to Hansen about Larry?"

"No. I'd like to get to him without Hansen or anybody else knowing. Maybe it's Rietman, maybe not. Maybe Rietman wasn't working alone."

"God almighty! That's a shitty feeling!"

"Let me have Larry's number and address."

"Oh, yeah." He unlocked the security drawer that held the files on the agents' confidential informants. "Here." He wrote the information on his memo from the desk of.

"You certain this is the right name?"

Johnston double-checked. "Yep—Larry Ginsdale."

"Does Hansen also list a C.I. named Oscar Pitkin?"

"Here's an Oscar. No last name, though."

Anybody could have got to the snitches; it didn't mean a thing that their names were tied to Billy. "Has Baca made bail yet?"

"No. His was set high because of the assault charge."

"Who has the case?"

"Kolagny."

That was good; with his four years as an assistant D.A., Kolagny was the unit's most experienced prosecutor. In another year or two, he would move to private practice where the money was; then the unit would have to start training another lawyer. "Who does Farnsworth have?"

"Steinman."

That was bad; the defense was more equal than the prosecution. "I'd better call Kolagny."

"Right. And listen—I mean this: you really done good last night. I appreciate it."

"Any time." Wager knew how Ed felt; a cop did things for other people—that was expected—but from what a cop learned of human nature, he was always surprised when someone else, even a fellow officer, did something for him. Gabe went back to his desk, where the first number he dialed was Larry's. No answer. He pushed the button for the local circuit and telephoned the assistant D.A. "Is Counselor Kolagny there? This is Detective Wager."

The lawyer wasted no time. "You're ready now? Come on over."

"Yes, sir."

The trip across the Civic Center Park to the City-County Building was short but cold; the gray building's east face was draped with ropes of Christmas lights that quivered and whistled in the icy wind. Even now, with the lights off, pedestrians crowded the sidewalk to gaze at the decorations. Wager turned in to a side door of the curving north wing and shrugged the hallway's warm air into his coat. Kolagny's office was an ex-storage closed jammed beneath the third-floor stairs and hot from the pipes that ran down one wall. A new justice center was being built, but even in the planning stage it was overcrowded, and the familiar rumors of cost overrun threatened more cuts in space. Wager wondered why ordinary civilians were required to honor contracts but builders on city projects weren't.

"Counselor?"

"Sit down, Detective Wager—watch your head."

He ducked the steam pipe and handed the lawyer his report. Kolagny, eyes slanted up at the corners by his high cheekbones, studied the sheets of handwriting. "You're certain they initiated the plan to run guns and to trade narcotics for the guns?"

"They brought up the idea, yes."

"Did you encourage them in any way?"

"I said I could get the guns and provide transportation."

"Did they at any time want to withdraw from the proposed scheme?"

"They talked about it. They thought it was pretty dangerous."

"Did you encourage them to continue?"

"I told them the guns were available only this once. That they might be better off not to do it if they thought it was too much for them. That if they did want to do it, it was now or never."

"That 'if they wanted to do it'?"

"Yes, sir; or words to that effect."

"It would be best to have the exact words, but don't try to add anything on the witness stand."

Wager had been testifying in court before Kolagny was in law school. "Yes, sir."

"When did you identify yourself as a police officer?"

"At the time of the arrest."

"Was that before or after Baca allegedly fired at you?"

Allegedly, hell. "After. Baca fired and I returned fire with one round. Then Ed yelled 'Police officer.'"

"Sergeant Johnston identified himself after you fired, and you did not identify yourself."

"I had other things on my mind."

"There goes the assault-on-an-officer charge. Baca did fire before you fired—you're certain of that."

"I am."

"Who drew his weapon first, you or Baca?"

"He did. My report covers that sequence."

"I realize that, Officer, but we don't have much time before the advisement, do we?" Kolagny jotted something in the margin of Wager's report. "We'll change that to aggravated assault and assault with a deadly weapon. Were any guns actually transferred as payment?"

"No, sir." Though that shouldn't make any difference. The statute was clear: selling, offering to sell or give, intent to sell or give were all the same violation.

"O.K., I think we have them. They'll ask for a motion to suppress the evidence, of course, but it looks good for possession and selling. And we should get Baca on the assault."

"We might get Farnsworth on that, too. He knew it was a rip-off, and he knew Baca was carrying iron."

"I appreciate your advice, Detective Wager, but let me draw up the formal charges, O.K? By the way—you're absolutely certain that the seized material is cocaine?"

"Sergeant Johnston ran a presumptive positive test."

"So did that other man in your unit—Rietman."

That was what credibility meant, and that was how far the damage could spread. "The official laboratory report should be ready this afternoon."

"Hmm." He scribbled again. "Well, just to be safe, I'll word the formal charge 'selling a drug of the cocaine family.' That should cover lidocaine or some other derivative."

"Yes, sir."

"Will you be at the advisement?"

Normally on a big bust he would be, but not today. "I have another case."

"I'll keep you posted."

Back in his own office, Wager tried Larry's number again; still no answer. He called the police laboratory and asked for Douglas. "Have you had a chance to test the stuff I brought in last night, Archie?"

"It's—let's see—fourth on the list. We'll get to it right after lunch."

"The advisement's this afternoon. Can you notify Kolagny as soon as possible?"

"Will do."

He turned to the current wave of paperwork and spent the rest of the morning shuffling envelopes from one pile to another. Every half-hour he tried Larry's number. At two, he finally got an answer. "Hello?"

"Is this Larry?"

"Who wants to know?"

"Gabe."

"The hard-ass? What the hell do you want?"

"You. I'll be over in fifteen minutes. Stay put."

"I don't want to see you!"

"Stay there—don't make me waste time looking for you, because I sure as hell will find you." He hung up and left a note on Suzy's typewriter: "On pager. Call Archie Douglas for lab report this P.M."

Larry's address was a narrow frame house on Ogden Street just off Eighth. Across the street rose an apartment's thirty floors like boxes set one above the other. On either side of Larry's two-story house, large brick homes had been cut into apartments and labeled "Ogden Arms" and "Rathbourne House." Neither of the sagging dark red homes lived up to its new name. Wager went up the creaking steps to the wooden front porch. Four metal mailboxes were nailed to the wall beside the cut-glass sidelight of the door. Downstairs right, Apartment 2: L. D. Ginsdale. The narrow hallway was bare of furniture and had that stale smell of rarely distrubed dust left under an old strip of worn carpet. The dark door of Apartment 2 rattled slightly as he knocked.

"Who is it?"

"Gabe."

"Just a minute." The lock scraped open and the door eased to the length of its short chain. Larry's brown eye peered at Wager. "What the hell do you want?"

"Inside, Larry. I got a deal you can't refuse."

"What kind of deal? I ain't laying you on anybody else. I didn't want to do that other shit in the first place."

"It's nothing like that. This is a real winner. All you got to do is hear it."

"Well, let's hear it."

"Not out here. Inside."

The eye blinked once, twice. Then the door swung shut and the chain slid off. Wager pushed into the room.

"What kind of deal?" He was looking at Wager with his head to one side, weighing, Gabe knew, the possibility of another crooked cop.

"I hear you're onto some MDA."

"You can't believe everything you hear."

"I believe this. I heard it from the guy you sold it to, Bruce the Juice."

"What are you after, man? You said something about a deal."

"The deal is this: I won't bust your ass for selling to Bruce if you tell me who your pipeline is."

"What pipeline? Hey, somebody's handing you a lot of crap!"

"You knew when the Nederland bust was coming. You tipped Bruce about it. I want to know where you got your information."

"That little bastard told you that?"

"He wanted to get his tail out of a crack—the same one your tail's in now."

"You got a warrant on me?"

"I hope I won't need one. It's not you I'm after."

Ginsdale ran a hand over his skull and tugged at the little fringe of oily curls on the back of his neck. "You won't hassle me?"

"I can get you right now for selling to Bruce. But I want that pipeline more than I want you."

His thin lips opened in what passed for a smile. "All right —I guess a crooked cop's worth more than me."

"It is a cop? You know him?"

"Shit, I should. Me and Oscar's been paying the son of a bitch for over a goddam year now. We know as much about what you people are doing as you do."

"It's in our office and not D.E.A?"

"I don't know nobody in D.E.A. But hell, they got their share, too; don't feel bad."

It wasn't Billy! By God, he knew all along it couldn't be Billy —he had said it from the first! Wager almost smiled, "All right; all right; now you just tell me all about Rietman."

"You got another crooked one?"

"What do you mean another one?"

"Man, I don't know any Rietman. The one I'm talking about is your buddy Hansen."

Wager said nothing, but a picture started falling together in his angry mind. Finally Ginsdale cleared his throat. "Now, we still got our deal, ain't we?"

"Yes. Where's your phone?" The radio pack was useless; Hansen was on the net.

Ginsdale pointed.

Wager dialed the O.C.D. number. Suzy answered. "This is Gabe. Is Hansen there?"

"Right here—you want to talk with him?"

"No! Give me Sergeant Johnston. And don't tell anyone, not even Hansen, that I called."

She was more surprised than puzzled, but she knew enough not to ask questions. "Yes, sir."

The sergeant's extension lifted. "Detective Sergeant John-ston."

"This is Gabe. Use Sonnenberg's safe line and call me back at this number." He read it to Johnston.

"Is it really important?"

"Jesus Christ, Ed!"

"O.K., O.K.—I just don't like interrupting him, you know?"

Larry's telephone rang a few seconds later.

"The C.I. says Hansen's our man. Play it cool—he's in the office now. Can you and Sonnenberg meet me at the Frontier in fifteen minutes?"

"I'll ask the inspector."

Sonnenberg's voice came on: "Is this C.I. reliable?"

"What he says sounds right. But you'll have to talk to him anyway."

"That's true. We'll see you there."

"In the back room." He hung up and motioned to Ginsdale. "Get your coat—you're going to talk to the inspector."

"Right now? I got things to do!"

"Move."

"Let me make a call. Will you let me make one call?"

"To who?"

The lump of Adam's apple rose and fell. "I got some business set up. They're expecting me in an hour."

"Does it have anything to do with Hansen?"

"No—it's just straight business."

"Keep it short and clean."

He dialed and muttered something as the rings continued. At last, "This is Larry—the deal's off for today. I'll call tomorrow at the same time." Wager heard the faint quack of an excited female voice. "No, I trust you, baby; but something's come up. I'll call tomorrow."

"Hang up," said Wager.

"I got to go—I'll call same time tomorrow."

Like hell he would. "Come on."

They waited in Wager's favorite booth near the now quiet serving window to the kitchen. At midafternoon, the only patrons in the bar area were a few businessmen and some mailmen grabbing quick beers on government time. The large back room was empty except for a pair of middle-aged lovers with no place else to meet.

"I never been here before. Jesus, look at all the junk they got around!" Ginsdale peered through the dim light of the wagon-wheel chandelier at the branding irons, old weapons, cowboy tackle, posters, and mining gear hung and labeled on every wall and halfway across the ceiling. "Are the other rooms like this, too?"

"Yes."

"Man, I got to come back here. Jesus, they even got a real cigar-store Indian."

"Yes."

The sergeant and the inspector finally came past the bar and Wager raised a hand. Sonnenberg ordered a beer from Rosie and studied Ginsdale. The sergeant ordered the same.

"Tell me all about it, Mr. Ginsdale."

"Yes, sir. Well, like I was telling Detective Wager here—that's your real name? Wager? I heard of you. Anyway, like I was telling him, me and this friend of mine started working for Officer Hansen just after we come in from the Coast."

"Informing?"

"Well, yeah, I guess you could call it that. He just wanted information and we let him know what was going down on the street. You know how it is."

"I know. Then what?"

"Well, me and Oscar, that's my buddy, we thought he was setting us up, you know? Maybe he didn't make his quota of busts for that month or something."

"When was this?" asked Wager.

"A little over a year ago. A year ago September. Anyway, at first it was mostly grass and not much of that. Then Hansen comes up with a little smack, and right away Oscar says, 'You're setting us up.' And Hansen swears he ain't and says he couldn't stick us anyway because we could plead entrapment. So me and Oscar talk it over and figure what the hell—we know as much about that entrapment crap as the next guy, and Hansen's right: we're clear. Besides"—again the gaping of lips that passed for a grin—"we figured that if the shit hit the fan, most of it would land on a rogue cop anyway. So we go into business—fifty percent for him, fifty for us."

Sonnenberg held a slightly quivering match to his cigar; in the yellow glare his mouth was a tight line. "Where did Hansen get the drugs?"

"He didn't say nothing except he got them cheap and that we should sell for less than market and move them quick. Hell, it was a gold mine anyway, so there wasn't no sense in being greedy." He finished his drink; Wager ordered another for him. "I think maybe the State of Colorado was his supplier, if you know what I mean."

They knew. "Six months ago," guessed Wager, "you went heavy into snort. Did Hansen supply it?"

"Jeez—where'd you hear about that? Yeah, one night we get a call and Hansen asks how fast can we move some coke. Well, you know, we have to find who's buying what, but it ain't hard. Not if you been around, anyway. So we call back the next night and say sure. The deal went down for half a kilo, man!" He stopped, eyes wide. "You know nobody's warned me of my rights—you can't use this on me!"

"It isn't you we want, Mr. Ginsdale. But we would like you to testify to this arrangement with Roger Hansen."

"Well, Detective Wager here said something about a deal."

"I said I'd forget that he sold some MDA if he helped us get a god damned crooked cop."

"Um." The inspector drew on his maduro. "I think your freedom's worth a little more help, Mr. Ginsdale."

"What kind of help?"

"I want you to arrange for one more buy."

"You mean this ain't enough what I'm telling you?"

The cigar pulsed. "It's enough for a case. But I want enough for a coffin to bury the son of a bitch in."

Wager could not remember the last time Sonnenberg swore; his eye caught Johnston's startled face.

"Well, Jesus, Inspector, I don't know. We just did a big . . . I mean, he usually calls us when he has something. He might not have nothing left."

"How much MDA did he supply?" guessed Wager again.

Ginsdale blinked. "You really been onto me! And I didn't even know it!"

"I got a lot more I can lay on you if I have to. How much did he supply?"

"Twenty pounds of pure. It was beautiful stuff."

Johnston grunted. "Well, sure! That's the stuff from the Springs!"

"He can get more if he wants to," said Wager. "How can you get a contact with him?"

"I can call him tonight. At home."

"He uses his own home phone?" For some reason Wager found that almost as shocking as the dishonesty.

"Yeah. We just say we got a buyer and he says when to get together."

"All right, it's almost four o'clock. We'll call and you'll tell him you've got a buyer for another ten pounds." Wager's words made Ginsdale's head sink a little. "What's wrong?"

"Well, my buddy Oscar. He's in this, too. You deal with me, you deal with him. That's the way it's got to be."

Wager raised his eyebrows at the inspector, who answered, "Fine. But don't misconstrue our arrangement, Mr. Ginsdale. We're not giving you a license to deal; we're just withholding current charges pending the outcome of this investigation. If you indulge in activities from now on, we will bring new charges. Is that clear?"

"I think so."

Wager said, "If you or Oscar push a half a gram, I'll bust your fucking asses."

"Oh—I hear you! No, we'll be clean. Count on it."

"Where's Oscar now?"

"Around."

"Call him. Tell him to get over to your place but don't tell him why. I'm going to sit with you two until the deal goes down. If that's all right with you, Inspector?"

"I think that's a good move. Mr. Ginsdale, how much will the payment to Hansen be?"

"We don't usually pay until after a deal."

"Just tell Hansen your buyer put up half and that you're giving it to him. We want to see Hansen take the money from you," said Wager.

"Oh, I get it. Well, it'll be about ten thousand, then. We sell it for two thousand dollars a pound. Nobody beats our prices, man."

Why not? It didn't cost them a damn thing. "Ed, can you bring it over? And maybe we ought to record the conversation."

"That won't do you no good in court, will it? I mean tapes ain't allowable evidence?"

"They are, Mr. Ginsdale, if one of the parties testifies to the accuracy of the recorded conversation."

"No shit!" He filed that item for future reference.

Wager stood. "Let's go call Oscar."


Oscar, younger than Ginsdale and with long heavy sideburns that made his round face even fatter, had only shrugged when Larry told him what was going on. "I ain't got no great affection for Detective Hansen," he said. "Larry's my buddy and he's got good smarts. If he made a deal, that's fine with me."

That meant they had already made enough to be glad to leave the state before they were busted. Wager paced across the small living room of Ginsdale's apartment. "You remember what I want you to say?"

"Sure, Gabe. It ain't much different from what we always say."

"Be sure and mention the MDA and the money. Ten thousand."

"Yeah, sure. You guys want a beer? We got beer in the box."

"No." Wager would like one. He was hungry, too. But he would enjoy his meal a lot more after the bust and after he was rid of these pukes.

The door rattled under a knock; Ginsdale looked at Wager.

"Ask who it is."

"Who is it?"

"Ed Johnston."

"Let him in."

Johnston puffed in carrying the portable recorder. "Sorry I took so long. The inspector thought we should get a court order for the recording. He don't want nothing going wrong on this."

When did he ever want anything going wrong? "Let's get set up."

The hookup was complete in five minutes. Gabe ran a test call to D.P.D. and played back the brief conversation. Then, "O.K., Ginsdale, do it."

The thin man finished his beer and cleared his throat. "Now?"

"Come on—come on!"

"All right, take it easy." He dialed; Wager verified the number in his notebook. Through the earphones, he heard Hansen say hello.

"Roger? This is Larry. I got a buyer for ten pounds of MDA. He's put up half the money. I can let you have your ten K now. Can you get the stuff tonight?"

That was fine, thought Wager: the identifying name and all the details of the transaction. Now, you bastard, answer right.

"Tonight?" Hansen's voice dropped. "No way can I get it

tonight. Tomorrow afternoon at the earliest."

Wager nodded yes to Ginsdale's inquiring glance.

"O.K. Where and when do we meet?"

"What's wrong with the same place?"

"Nothing. That's fine. The same place. When?"

"Is something wrong?"

"Wrong? No! Things are cool, real cool. Why?"

"You don't sound the same."

Wager made cutting signals across his throat.

"Everything's O.K., man; I'm in a hurry's all."

"O.K. Let's do it at two. I'll see you there."

The line clicked into a buzz.

"Well," asked Johnston, "what do we do now, drop back and punt?"

"We do what we have to," said Wager. And that meant spending another fifteen hours cooped up with scum like Ginsdale and Pitkin. He sighed and picked up the telephone, dialing a familiar number. "How do you people like your pizza?"

Pitkin looked up from tuning the television set. "I don't like pizza."

"That means with mushrooms," said Wager, and ordered one large for them and one separate small one for himself.

"You saying we can't leave?" Ginsdale's voice wanted to squeak.

"No leaving, no calls until after you meet Hansen."

"Aw, you got to be kidding, man!"

"Try me."

Johnston stood and whispered under the noise of the television, "You want some relief? A partner?"

"We'd better not. Hansen knows people all over the department. All we have to do is get the word out that we're sitting on these two cruds and there goes the whole thing."

"But there's two of them."

"They've got as much to lose by messing up. They'll sit here."

186

"Then why do you need to stay here?"

"Because they're dumb, Ed, and Ginsdale's about to rupture because he wants to finish one last deal. They might do something that would accidentally tip Hansen."

"Right. Well, listen, is there anything I can get for you?"

"Send a cold six-pack. I don't even like drinking their crap. And did Archie Douglas send over the lab report on that dope from last night?"

"Seventy-eight percent cocaine. About as good as most labs produce."

"That'll tickle Kolagny. How did the advisement go?"

"Farnsworth made bail, Baca didn't. They both entered a motion to suppress."

"It figures." That meant at least six weeks before the judge would hear arguments on suppression of evidence. From there, it would be another month to the preliminary hearing to determine if they'd be bound over for trial. Then a maximum six months before the guilty sons of bitches were brought in for their fair trial. Except, of course, for continuances asked by the defendants. And finally the appeals following the trial. In a year or so, they would go to jail. Wager rubbed a hand over the weary flesh of his face: it was lawyer Kolagny's game from here out; Gabe was now just another pawn. Which was fine with him—he was tired, and he still had Hansen.

Pitkin wanted Chinese food for lunch—the pizza had given him gas all night, he said, and he didn't know why in the hell Wager went ahead and ordered that wop food when he told him he didn't like it. Across the little boxes whose wet-cardboard smell spoke to Wager of hundreds of meals eaten in parked cars, in run-down hotel rooms, even at his desk, Ginsdale sucked bean sprouts until Wager, his appetite fading into the weariness of a too light sleep on a too short couch, finally stood. "It's time."

It was a brief drive across town to the empty parking lot of

187

the McNichols Arena, a squat mushroom of concrete that loomed just west of I-25. Larry drove; Oscar sat beside him. Wager was in the back seat by himself.

"Pull over at the next corner."

"This all right?"

"Fine." He saw Johnston angle to the curb behind them. The inspector got out and walked to Larry's car; the radio pack was still useless with the suspect tied into the net.

"Everything set, Gabe?"

"Mr. Ginsdale don't like wearing the body transmitter. Other than that, we're all right."

"Think of it as your contribution to a cleaner Denver, Mr. Ginsdale."

"Yes, sir, Inspector. Ha-ha."

"We're set, too, Gabe."

He got out and leaned to the driver's window one last time. "Just play it like it's for real. When he gives you the MDA, you hand him the money and say, 'Have a good day.' That's the bust signal: 'Have a good day.'"

"You sure this gismo works? I hear a lot about them breaking down."

"It works. Especially in an open parking lot." He started to go, and then said, "Oh—and don't go anywhere with that MDA. Just stay in your car until Sergeant Johnston gets to you. Clear?"

"Yeah, yeah."

"Give us five, then go in."

They pulled the unmarked car into an ice-streaked alley that had a clear view of the wide asphalt lot. It was empty. A few moments later, Larry and Oscar drove their Impala slowly across the old snow and coasted to a halt near the center. Johnston balanced the binoculars on the steering wheel and fiddled with the focus screw. The receiver of the Kell Kit body transmitter squawked, "Here he comes."

"Right," said Ed. "He's just turning in."

In the back seat, Wager switched on the tape recorder. They watched the O.C.D.'s unmarked Plymouth crackle through the puddles of melting snow.

Larry's voice came over the microphone, "You set?"

Oscar might have said "Yeah," but the signal was too broken to tell.

"They're getting out," said Ed. "So's Hansen."

"We can see that, Sergeant. Just keep your eyes on the dope."

"Yes, sir."

"Hi, Rog. . . . Yeah, I got the money right here. . . . That's good, the MDA looks real good. . . . O.K., and, ah, have a good day."

"Now," said the inspector. Johnston pulled from the alley and swung around the fence into the entryway, the car whining into second gear as they splashed toward the three men turning to watch them arrive. Johnston skidded to a halt; Sonnenberg was out of the car before it stopped rocking, and Gabe was just behind him, eyes fixed on Hansen's gun hand.

"Inspector! What are you guys doing here?"

"It's all over, Hansen. Let's go in."

"What's all over? What the hell are you people talking about?" To Wager, he looked like a kid caught with his hand in the cookie jar, determined to bluff it out, determined that they would believe him if he only sounded innocent enough.

"You know your rights, Hansen? Or do you want them read?"

"Inspector, I don't know what the shit you think this is. I don't know what the shit game you people think you're playing!"

Sergeant Johnston said to Larry, "Let's have it."

He handed the sergeant a paper sack; Ed looked in it.

"And the Kell Kit."

Larry propped a foot on his car's bumper and unstrapped the small flat box from his bony shin. Then he drew the mike cord up through his trousers and out of his grimy shirt collar. Hansen watched him.

Larry turned to the inspector. "Now what?"

"Now go home. Stay clean—stay in town until you get an O.K. from us to leave."

Then Sonnenberg said, "Hansen, hand over your weapon and the money."

"Inspector, I honest to God don't—"

Wager lunged, both hands gripping for the open collar of Hansen's topcoat, spinning the larger detective around and grabbing the handle of the policeman's weapon through the heavy cloth. "All right, you son of a bitch, if you want it this way—spread; God damn your soul, spread! You're busted!"

"Aw, shit! Aw, shit, shit, *shit!*" Hansen's voice cracked and so did he, leaning heavily against the side of his car, knees sagging and forehead jammed against the car roof gutter. "Shit. Here." He held out the roll of marked bills. "No cuffs. You got me."

The interrogation took place in the inspector's office. Hansen, who seemed almost glad to be caught, waived his right to an attorney. He spoke directly to the tape recorder's microphone; he did not look up at either Wager or Johnston. Occasionally, he looked across the desk at the inspector and said, "You see?"

"Where did you get your supply?"

"In the custodian's office. Most of it was dope that had been used as evidence and then stored after the trial ended. Everybody just forgot about it; it never was even inventoried. It was just so goddamn easy—the stuff just sat there and nobody ever checked it. You see?"

"How did you get access to the custodian's office?"

"Well, I—ah—well, I didn't. Liz got it for me."

"Last name?" The inspector motioned to Johnston, who nodded.

"Miller. She's a civilian employee there."

Johnston left the room.

"Not a police officer?" asked Wager. He remembered the woman with hair longer than regulations allowed.

Hansen hunched his shoulders. "No. Not an officer."

"Tell us about it," said Sonnenberg.

"Well, it was easy. She'd get the stuff and I'd come by for coffee. Then we would sit down, and she'd just leave it on the table when she left. I'd pick it up and walk out."

"What about a ten-pound package of MDA? She didn't just walk out of the custodian's office with ten pounds of dope!"

"Yes, sir. That was her lunch bag. Nobody ever looked, you see?"

"Jesus Christ," said Wager. "Ten pounds of lunch!"

"Yeah." Hansen almost laughed, but stifled it. "If it wasn't so easy, I wouldn't of tried it."

"Now." Sonnenberg pinched his cigar and leaned forward. "What about Rietman? Was he in this with you?"

"No, sir. That was a fuck-up. His evidence got put in the post-trial section instead of the pre-trial section, and we—Liz —made the switch with some lactose. Boy, was I surprised when I heard what happened."

Wager almost spit through the acid taste on the back of his tongue. "So was Rietman."

"Yeah. Well. There wasn't much I could say at the time."

Sonnenberg scribbled a note to himself. "What was your reason?"

"I don't know. Money. Me and my wife's been having troubles lately. And, well, me and Liz, we got a thing going. I don't know; it seemed like the thing to do at the time, you see? We'd get enough bread to split for South America. God, there's a lot of money just sitting in that custodian's office, and it was so easy—security ain't much good there."

"There will be changes made," said Sonnenberg.

Sergeant Johnston knocked and entered. "D.P.D.'s been given a warrant on her, sir."

The inspector grunted and turned back to Hansen. "Anything else you want to add? Anything you want to say?"

Hansen shrugged again. "I guess I said it all. Do you have to put me in custody? I sent some people up, you know, and they're still in."

They all knew how long a cop would last in jail. "You volunteered a confession; I think we can ask for low bail."

"Thank you, sir."

Sonnenberg sighed and drew on his cigar. Wager tried to hide a yawn; as he had listened, as he had watched, the muscles of his neck and back had slowly relaxed and the eight hours' sleep of the last three days began to catch up with him. He still had to call Billy and tell the D.E.A. agent when Ginsdale and Pitkin were leaving the state. Billy didn't need to know that the tip was an apology.

The inspector pushed the rewind button on the tape recorder. "At least Officer Rietman gets a Christmas present out of this."

"I don't know if it'll do any good," said Sergeant Johnston. "I heard he resigned. He's moving back East somewhere."

"I see." The inspector did not look at Hansen. "Take this one over to the bail commissioner."

Wager and Hansen met Gargan in the lobby of the City-County Building; the reporter smelled a story and stared hard at Roger. "What's going down, Gabe? Can you tell me something about it?"

"Gabe," Hansen mumbled, "I wish you wouldn't."

Wager looked at the ex-cop and did not feel a thing. No pleasure, no pity. And maybe Rietman would be interested in the story. "It's all public now, Hansen. Even this."

# 13

Outside the window beside Wager's desk, the heavy spring snow had finally stopped, and by midmorning the sun seemed to glare from every direction: above, below, even from under the window's overhang where the brilliance made the normally dusty shadows a clear blue. The streets were already wet black strips of tire tracks, and the heat of a March sun would soon melt the rest of the thick snow. Wager wagged his head at the telephone's mouthpiece. "O.K., Fat Willy—where and when?"

The wheezing voice said, "Nineteenth and Wazee—there's this Mexican joint. You know about them spic joints, don't you, Señor Wager?"

"I know. What time?"

"Ten. There's two cunts. We getting a lot of them in the business lately."

"Well, it's a democracy, Willy."

"Yeah—if you white, hey, brother?"

"I'll see you at ten."

"Hey, I heard ol' Roger the Dodger's got his day in court today."

Wager glanced at the squeaking electric clock on a filing cabinet; the preliminary was in a half-hour. Johnston and Wager had been told to attend just in case. "That's right."

"Well give ol' Rog a big kiss for me. And, say, if you ever get a little extra stuff you want to sell, I won't turn fink like them two honkies."

"Not likely, Willy." Not very God damned likely.

"Don't shit me, man; all you fuzz is the same—give a crook a badge and call him a cop. Haw!"

"Ten tonight, Willy."

"Right on. Brother. Haw!"

He hung up. "Suzy, I'm on pager at Hansen's preliminary."

"All right, Gabe." She watched him pass the green plywood partition.

"You ready, Ed?"

"Right. The inspector's coming, too." Johnston smoothed down his strands of red hair and cocked the narrow-brimmed hat over his right eye. Like the inspector's, it was dark green; but the feather in the hatband was a shade smaller.

The walk to the courtroom was wet, many of the sidewalks packed into icy slush and not yet scraped clean. Each corner was backed up with pools of muddy water. The three men were silent until they finally eased into one of the blond wooden benches of the courtroom. In the empty jury box sat three men waiting their arraignment; they had that thin, gray look that comes with prison. Hansen, out on bail, sat with his lawyer on a front bench. He did not look around as Wager and the others came in.

"Did you have your talk with Rietman, sir?" asked Johnston

as they peeled off their topcoats. "Is he still quitting?"

The inspector's voice was level. "Yes. He told us to go to hell. He wants nothing more to do with D.P.D. or anyone in it."

"Oh. That's too bad. He didn't have to tell us to go to hell, though."

"I deserved it. It was my mistake. I should have held a formal hearing instead of transferring him."

"I guess so. But it wasn't very respectful."

The inspector changed the subject. "I hear Farnsworth pleaded guilty."

"Yes, sir," said Wager. "But the sentencing was something else."

It was a first conviction; Farnsworth had been given a suspended sentence. If he was a nice boy for three years, the sentence would be dropped. Hell, with the money he had stashed away from his dealing, anybody could be a nice boy for three years.

"He was smart to try for the lesser charge."

That had been Ramona's idea, and Kolagny—up to his ears in cases—had bought it. Wager could still see her and little Peter sitting behind the defendant's table across the aisle. Hatred made her eyes wet; Peter's eyes were puzzled and afraid. Somehow, Uncle Gabe, who had given him a Christmas present, had turned out to be an enemy, and his mama had smashed the present and mailed it back. Uncle Gabe was a cop, and cops were enemies and hurt Daddy and made Mama get mad and cry. Worse than anything were cops who pretended to be friends. Wager could see the question in Pedro's eyes. Why did he have to hurt Mama and Daddy? Would he hurt me? When? And how could Wager tell a kid that his mother would have been on trial, too, except that she was smarter than his old man? "Yes, sir."

"When's Baca's trial?"

He had pleaded not guilty, and Kolagny decided not to bargain on that one, because Chicanos were easier to convict. "August, sir."

They lapsed into silence as the bailiff called Hansen's case. The motion to suppress his confession had been heard and denied; and Hansen's lawyer, still angry at his client's waiving his right to an attorney during interrogation, had not told Kolagny what his plea would be. The bailiff read the charges and the judge asked if the defendant understood them.

"Yes, Your Honor, he does."

"How does the defendant plead?"

"The defendant pleads guilty as charged, Your Honor, and begs that the court in sentencing consider that the defendant's life would be in jeopardy if he is confined to prison."

The judge finished noting the plea on his form and studied his calendar. "So noted. The defendant will remain free on bail, if prosecution has no strenuous objection. Sentencing is set for . . . April 18th." He marked his calendar. "Next."

"How about that?" asked Johnston. "I was sort of hoping he'd plead not guilty." They filed out and stood a moment in the tall, echoing hall outside the frosted glass doors labeled "Court Room Three." Hansen came out and quickly turned to talk with his lawyer as he walked past the three men.

"What do you think he'll get, Inspector?" asked Johnston.

"It's a first offense, and a jail sentence would be a death sentence. Probably the same as Farnsworth."

That was what Wager thought, too. The law was supposed to be applied equally to all similar offenders. But to Wager's mind, a crook who said he was a crook wasn't nearly as bad as a cop who turned out to be a crook. There were a lot of things the law wasn't worth a damn on.

"Well"—Sonnenberg rolled the tip of his cigar in the match flame—"he's got a wife and kids, too. And it was a lot of money. Anybody might be tempted by that much money."

Wager disagreed with the inspector on that. There were cops with pride—men with pride—who tried not to play games with their lives or anyone else's.